OUT
OF THE
DARKNESS

AMANDA K. MANN

OUT OF THE DARKNESS

A Dark Wolf Shifter Romance

AMANDA K. MANN

Out of the Darkness

Paperback ISBN: 979-8-9902675-2-7

Hardcover ISBN: 979-8-9902675-3-4

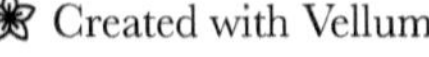 Created with Vellum

Prologue

He took a sip of beer from beneath his hood, his eyes tracking her every move. Sitting in the far corner booth, he had his back to the wall to prevent anyone from sneaking up on him. He also used the dim lighting and his hood to hide his identity, all out of habit. They were little quirks he had picked up from his previous line of work. However, it came in handy now as he had been able to watch her for the last several hours while going completely unnoticed.

The more he saw, the more he studied her, the more he wanted her, and the beast inside of him agreed. Everything about her was captivating as hell; the way her smile revealed an adorable set of dimples, how animated she got when she spoke about something she was passionate about. Then there was the way that she pushed her hair back behind her ear when she was nervous and the way she chewed on her bottom lip when she was deep in thought. The list went on and on. He knew the moment she walked into the bar that she was meant to be his, and she was *going* to be. Even if she didn't know it yet.

He had heard of this phenomenon before, a long time

ago, but the way it was talked about had him believing that it was just a myth or a legend. That it wasn't real. And even if it *was* real, he never thought it would happen to him. He was a beast, a monster of the worst kind, and he had more blood on his hands than he cared to admit due to killing people for a living. However, there was no denying the onslaught of emotions that were flooding through him now. The primal urge, the sudden need, the undeniable… *obsession*.

Nothing in this sick and twisted world mattered anymore, only her. Everything else faded away to the dark depths of his mind until only she remained. Well, her and his raging erection. That hadn't gone anywhere. If anything, that had only gotten more prominent the longer he was forced to watch her from afar and imagine what it would feel like to be buried deep inside of her as he claimed her as his. It was borderline painful, but the pain kept him grounded, kept the monster at bay. It was also the only thing keeping him from turning the small bar into a bloody massacre, even though she'd be worth it.

She was tiny, probably only about 5'4", and she had creamy pale skin with just a small smattering of freckles across her cheeks and her adorable button nose. She had plump, rosy lips, chestnut brown hair that went to the middle of her back, and these big green eyes that made him feral.

He noticed that she also had a small dove tattoo on her right wrist, which prompted him to give her the nickname "little dove." So sweet, so innocent, and a beacon of light in his otherwise dark and bloody life. Though, her low-cut shirt gave him a perfect view of her glorious tits, and the way her jeans clung to her ass would make any man with eyes drool. Granted, he would then have to gouge out those eyes with a rusty knife for looking at his girl, but that was beside the point.

To him, his little dove was perfect in every way, and soon, she would be all his. He would have approached her the moment she walked in instead of watching her from the shadows—if it were not for one pesky detail. His little dove was on a date with someone else.

The guy she was with wasn't even close to being good enough for her and was obviously not her type. He looked like a model who had to pad the front of his underwear with a roll of socks, and he was probably just as idiotic. He could tell that the two of them hadn't been together very long as they were still trying to get to know each other too. She wasn't completely comfortable with her date yet, but trying to fix that was a pointless effort since there wouldn't be another one after this. He didn't know what she saw in the guy, but it wouldn't be a problem after tonight. He'd make sure of it. And it looked like it was finally time to get this show on the road.

As the two of them got up and started gathering their belongings, he tossed some cash onto the table and moved toward the door himself. He wanted to get a head start so that it would make following them easier.

The air was drastically cooler outside with a few storm clouds rolling in as he made his way to his truck. He climbed into the driver's seat and adjusted the rearview so that he could keep an eye on the door. A few moments later, they emerged hand in hand. He ground his teeth in jealousy as the guy opened the car door for her and she gave him a shy yet sexy smile. He should be the one who had her smiling like that. He just kept reminding himself, and his monster, that she would be his soon enough.

Within moments, they were pulling out onto the highway, and he wasn't too far behind. He continued to follow at a safe distance as the man drove her back to her place. It was a cute little house that was rather secluded as it sat nestled into a little outcropping of trees that lined the forest. It wasn't very safe for a woman living alone, he noticed. Any monster with evil intentions could waltz right up to it without any witnesses, which would work out perfectly for him. He made a note of her address in his phone before watching the two of them say goodnight.

He nearly shifted on the spot when the asshole dared to kiss her, his wolf wanting to tear the guy apart with his teeth so he could feel the skin and muscle rip while the bones and tendons crunched and snapped. Those lips were his. *She* was his. As soon as he got this guy alone, he was going to pay for that.

Bloodlust consumed every fiber of his being as he followed his target back to his place. It was a little closer to town than he would have liked, but he would make due. He had been in more complicated situations before, and he had gotten very adept at adapting to the situation. Already, a plan was forming in his mind, and how he was going to make this guy pay made him giddy with excitement. He wasn't going to kill him, even though he definitely deserved it, but there were other, more creative ways to get his point across.

He was unfortunately bound by the vow he had made to himself, the one that forbade him from killing anymore unless it was absolutely necessary. There had been enough bloodshed, and he was trying *not* to go too far off the deep end. He had been doing this a long time now, so he had more than a few tricks up his sleeve that would still give him the same sense of satisfaction and satiate his bloodlust. His vow not to kill didn't prevent him from seriously maiming.

After pulling up across the street and killing the engine,

he picked his cell phone up out of the center console. He had a bit of time before he planned on going in, wanting the guy to feel nice and safe tucked away in his home, so he decided to see what kind of information he could gather in the meantime. He pulled up an app and quickly typed in the address. Once he had the guy's name, everything else was easy to find. He was like an open book.

David Carlisle, age twenty-eight. His parents were Stephen and Martha Carlisle. As an only child, he spent all his life in prestigious private schools and had everything handed to him on a silver platter. Now, he was a low-level lawyer at a law firm in town and was actually allergic to cats. He had learned that from David's dating profile, which had been all too easy to find. It was amazing what kind of weird tidbits someone would post to things like that.

After hacking into David's profile, he discovered that that's where he met her, Madelyn Hart. His little dove. He didn't know why she felt the need to be on a dating app in the first place as she was far too good for any of the sleaze-balls on it, but after a few moments, he found himself hacking into her profile as well. After all, he didn't need to know much about David. Once he got his point across, he would never see the guy again. Madelyn, however, was a different story, and he wanted to know everything there was to know about her.

According to her profile, she was twenty-five, nine years younger than he was. She loved hiking and being outdoors, loved to garden, and was obsessed with reading. It didn't say what she did for a living, but that would be easy enough for him to figure out.

He ended up losing track of time, saving all of her photos to his phone and scrolling through the messages guys had been sending her, each one pissing him off more than the last. They were animals, every one of them, and he eventually just deleted the whole damn thing. She wasn't going to need it anymore now that she had him.

Once that was done, he tossed his phone back into the center console and climbed out into the cool night air. It was time to get to work and show David what happened when he touched something that didn't belong to him. It was true that David had no idea that Madelyn was his, but after tonight, he most certainly would.

It was funny how trusting guys like David were. The back door wasn't even locked, and there was no security system either. So, he was able to slip inside completely undetected, his boots barely making a sound on the pristine tile floor. He could hear David in the bathroom, either washing his face or brushing his teeth, he wasn't sure. Either way, he only had a few moments to enact his plan.

Without so much as a rustle of clothing, he crept into the basement and found the breaker box in the far corner. The door creaked a bit as he opened it, but David didn't seem to hear it over the sound of the sink. Then, with a simple flip of a switch later, the house was shrouded in total darkness where his monster preferred to thrive.

"What the hell?" he heard David mutter from the bathroom.

A menacing smile graced his lips as he slipped into the dark corner behind the door and waited for David to come downstairs.

Usually, he preferred a bit more of a chase instead of just ambushing his targets from the shadows. He liked it when they were afraid as it made the job that much sweeter. But as this was a spur-of-the-moment thing, he was going to have to compromise a bit. He also realized that he was going to have to improvise some kind of weapon as well because his were all in a duffel bag at the bottom of his closet.

This wasn't like him. He was usually vastly over-prepared for things like this. However, his little dove was getting under his skin far more than he realized, and he was beginning to act irrationally. The thought made him smile as he couldn't wait to do the same to her.

A few agonizing moments later, David finally shuffled into view. David had taken a shower while he was waiting in the car, obsessing over his new girl. David's hair was still wet, and he was only wearing a pair of white underwear. He nearly laughed out loud at the sight. Real men at least wore boxer briefs. What this guy was currently wearing made him look like a pussy.

He closed his eyes for only a moment, but when he opened them again, the human in him was completely suppressed, leaving only the monster behind.

Slowing his breath and loosening his muscles, he waited until David began examining the breaker box, bent at the waist and using his cell phone as a flashlight. With the stealth and grace of an experienced predator, he struck fast, slamming David's head against the concrete wall. It wasn't hard enough to knock him out; he wanted David conscious for what he had planned, but it was just hard enough to daze and confuse the hell out of the guy.

He snatched a handful of David's hair and yanked his head back. He then snarled in his ear, sounding far more animal than man. The beast inside of him was in charge now. He was the one running the show, and the beast was *pissed*.

"W-who are you?" David stammered. "What do you want?"

There were all manner of ways in which he could answer that, but he decided to go with the most reasonable response. "You and I are going to have a chat, David," he sneered before he shoved him back toward the middle of the room. "About Madelyn."

"Madelyn?" David asked, lifting a shaky hand to the now-open and bleeding wound on his head. The surprise was evident in his voice, and his brows creased in confusion. Though it could also have been the blow he took to the head.

"Uh-huh."

"W-what about her?"

He took a step toward David, who instinctively stepped away. His self-preservation instincts must have started kicking in. Maybe he wasn't as dumb as he looked. However, he wasn't going to get off that easily. He was in for far more than just a stern talking-to.

He cocked his head to the side as if studying David. He still couldn't see what Madelyn saw in him. David was weak, pathetic, and no good for her. Not that he was any better. But between the two of them, he was by far the superior choice.

"You are going to stay the fuck away from her," he stated casually. "You aren't going to call her; you aren't going to text her; you aren't going to see her. You are going to disappear from her life altogether, starting right now."

"What, are you, her boyfriend or something?" David asked, shaking his head. "Look, man, she told me she was single. I have no desire to get in between—"

He chuckled darkly. "No, I'm not her boyfriend. Not yet anyway. But I don't need someone like you getting in my way. Madelyn is mine."

It was then that the little weasel seemed to grow some balls. After processing what he had said, David took a step toward him and looked as though he were going to poke him in the chest. He must have thought better of it though, which was good because he was at least three times David's size. He would have bitten that finger off like it was a baby carrot.

"Now, wait just a damn minute," he began. "You don't get to break in here and tell me who I can and can't see. It would be different if you were already with her, but the fact that—"

He didn't allow David to finish his statement before he reared back and clocked him hard in the jaw with his fist. Already, he was sick of listening to the guy talk because he clearly didn't have anything important to say.

"I wasn't fucking asking, David!" he roared angrily, making David flinch and tremble.

Now was not the time to push him as he was barely holding it together. His wolf wanted to feel the crunch of cartilage and bone as he tore his throat out with his powerful jaws. He wanted to feel the warm spray of his blood as he watched the life drain from his eyes. Being rogue meant having an insatiable bloodlust, and it would be all too easy to quench that desire right here, right now. But that wasn't why he was here. He only wanted David to back off and stay away from Madelyn. He didn't think that was too much to ask.

Even though he could clearly see how close to losing it he was, David didn't seem to want to back down. He would have been impressed, if not for the guy's lack of clothing.

"Who Madelyn dates isn't up to you. It's her choice," David told him. He was obviously trying to appear confident, but the quiver in his voice gave him away. It always did. "And she chose me. So, you can take your petty-ass jealousy and get the hell out of my house before I call the police."

He grinned menacingly. He had been hoping David

would say something like that. It made the monster inside of him giddy with anticipation of what came next.

"Wrong answer," he spat. Then, he struck as quick and precise as a viper.

He moved so quickly that David didn't have time to react at all. He slammed the guy hard against the wall while simultaneously snatching up the first thing he could find on one of the shelves to use as a weapon. As they were in the basement, the only thing he found was a tool. A Phillips-head screwdriver to be exact.

In his own defense, he was restraining himself fairly well. Before he made the vow to himself to kill less, he would have ripped David's chest open with his bare hands and crushed his heart in his palm. It wasn't his fault that David decided to struggle against him. Otherwise, the screwdriver would have gone into his upper thigh where it was intended to go.

Instead, the weapon found its way to where the sun don't shine, sliding into the soft flesh right between the guy's ball sack and asshole as easily as a knife went into softened butter. He felt something snap, a tendon or nerve perhaps, and the warm trickle of blood and piss on his hand as David wet himself.

The wails that pierced the air were inhuman, and he almost felt bad for the guy. He may be a monster, but there were lines even he wouldn't cross. Messing with another guy's family jewels was one of them. David would be lucky if his dick ever worked right again. Whatever had snapped when he stabbed him sounded awfully important.

Even so, the beast inside of him let out a groan of appreciation. He had come to thrive off the pain of others, especially if he was the one to inflict it. He may have gone a little further than expected, but it would get his point across nonetheless.

He met David's eyes, allowing his own to glow with his shifter power. His canines elongated as his monster began to emerge fully. He was reveling in the fear that now permeated the air around them.

David's face was contorted in pain, streaked with snot and tears, and he also seemed to be fighting unconsciousness.

"I am only going to say this once, asshat. So, listen close," he growled, his voice low. "Madelyn is mine. She will *always* be mine. And if I ever see you around her again, I won't stop at mutilating your manhood. I will finish what I started and send you to whatever god you believe in. Do we understand each other?"

Once again, he had to give the guy credit where credit was due. He had to be in excruciating pain, but David still nodded rapidly. Or as much as he could with his arm pinning him against the wall by his throat.

He yanked the screwdriver out with a sickening yet satisfying sound, causing David to scream again. When he finally released him, David collapsed to the floor in a heap, trying to stem the bleeding with his hands while curling into the fetal position.

Moving to where David had dropped his cell phone, he kicked it back toward him and left the basement without another word. It was up to David to get himself some help —he didn't care either way. Nor was he worried about the guy calling the police on him. He knew how to cover his tracks, and David never saw his face due to the hood he kept over his head.

The night air greeted him like an old friend as he emerged from the back door, a smile on his face. Now that he got David out of the way, Madelyn was his for the taking. He would give her time to get over the guy, of course, but then, all bets were off.

Chapter One

Madelyn

Madelyn Hart was fighting the urge to break every traffic law known to man. As it was, she was already weaving in and out of traffic way more than was recommended and was pissing a lot of people off along the way if their blaring horns and middle fingers were anything to go by. She just didn't have the time or patience to care.

She had just been informed a half-hour ago that David, the guy she had recently started seeing and was actually developing some real feelings for, had been attacked in his home the night before and was now in the hospital. They hadn't given her any other information, but she knew it had to be bad. Otherwise, David would have called her and told her what was going on himself—or at least had the hospital do so. Since he hadn't, and she had to hear from one of their mutual friends, she was only able to guess what had transpired. That thought alone had her pushing her foot further down on the gas pedal.

This was all new to her, caring about someone else in this way. Madelyn wasn't a relationship kind of girl. She never had been due to what she had gone through as a child. That trauma had made it so she had some major trust issues, especially when it came to men. Every man in her life had betrayed her at some point, in some of the worst possible ways, and, growing up, she only knew fear and heartache. It had broken her, skewed her way of thinking, but she had vowed to never let anyone hurt her like that again.

That was why she was usually drawn to the 'bad boys', the ones with a million red flags who were only looking to hook up. Those guys were good for some hot and dirty sex and nothing more, and that was also the only time she let anyone be rough with her without fighting back. She found that some pain during sex was fun, and she happened to like it rough.

But those guys, the kind she usually went for, were definitely not relationship material, and she preferred it that way. She knew she was messed up, probably even broken beyond repair, but she had come to grips with that fact a long time ago, had learned to live with it.

A few months ago though, her best friend convinced her to try something new. Melanie pointed out how sad and lonely her life was and suggested that she step out of her comfort zone a bit and try to make some more meaningful connections. She had tried to resist, but Melanie was insistent. Thus, Madelyn created her very first dating profile.

Madelyn met David through that dating app a month ago. She had been apprehensive at first, but the more they hung out, the more she realized that they actually hit it off pretty well. David was tame compared to the other guys she had hooked up with, safe even, which was exactly what Melanie said she needed. None of them could have foreseen this happening though. Nor did she anticipate the turmoil it caused inside of her.

Butterflies swarmed in her stomach as the nurse led her to David's room in the ICU. As they made their way down the hall, she found herself wondering if she should have stopped somewhere to get him some flowers or those 'get well' balloons. They may not have put a label on it, but she was pretty sure that they were dating. It probably looked terrible, her showing up empty-handed, but there was no going back now that she had already made it this far. She was just going to have to make it up to him some other way. Obviously, she wasn't good at this kind of thing.

"Here you are, Ms. Hart," the nurse stated, motioning toward a closed door on the right of the hall.

Madelyn gave her an uneasy smile. "Thank you."

She watched as the nurse headed back the way they had come before she turned back to the room. Chewing on her lip, she took a moment to mentally prepare herself for what she might be walking in on. This was why she didn't allow herself to catch feelings. She felt like she was on an emotional rollercoaster without the ability to get off and she didn't like it. Add to that the fact that she hated hospitals and, internally, she was a complete wreck.

Knowing that she couldn't stand out in the hallway forever, she took a deep breath to calm some of her rampaging nerves before opening the door. It was a private room overlooking the woods with its own private bathroom as well. Several wooden cabinets lined the walls, and there were more than a few machines surrounding the single bed, which sat in the middle of the left wall.

David was in that bed, seemingly lost in thought. He

was lying back against the pillows, his blond hair tousled, as he stared out the window. He was hooked up to an IV, a heart rate monitor, a pulse ox machine, and a blood pressure cuff. However, apart from a small wound on his forehead and a bruise on his jaw, he seemed relatively unharmed.

Madelyn breathed a sigh of relief, now knowing that it wasn't life-threatening. It felt like a weight lifted off of her shoulders, and she was grateful for it.

David must have heard her then because he finally turned his gaze over toward her and the door. She smiled at him in response as she made her way to his bedside. "I'm sorry I wasn't here sooner," she told him softly. She set her purse on the chair by the bed before reaching for his hand. "I came as soon as I heard. How are you feeling? Are you—"

"Don't," David suddenly sneered, snatching his hand away from her as if her touch had burned him.

Her brows furrowed as she stiffened, and she realized that he had never looked at her that way before. It was a look of disgust and disdain, and it felt like a slap to the face.

"David, what—"

"You need to leave, Madelyn," he told her angrily. "Now. We're done. Do you hear me? We are fucking done."

"Why? What did I do?" she asked, shaking her head. None of this was making any sense to her. She had just seen the guy last night, and things had been damn near perfect. Now, all of a sudden, they were done? Just like that?

"What did you do?" David screamed, causing her to jump.

His eyes were crazed, full of rage—and something else.

Something she couldn't put her finger on. It was as if whatever happened had changed him in such a way that she didn't even recognize him anymore.

Yanking the blankets off of his lap, he then motioned toward his crotch. "You're the fucking reason I'm here! You're the reason that fucking psycho came after me and made it so I can't have a normal fucking sex life! You ruined my fucking life!"

Madelyn blinked at him, still trying to process what he was saying to her. Then, her gaze moved down, and that was when she noticed the bandage between his legs. The skin around the bandage appeared to be bruised, and there was a bloodstain on the gauzy material. Whatever had happened to him had been personal, and it had to have hurt, but that still didn't explain how any of this was her fault.

It was then that she finally deciphered what that other emotion was that she saw behind his eyes. It was fear. He was afraid of her. But why?

"I'm… I'm sorry this happened to you. Really, I am," she told him after a while. "But David, I had nothing to do with this."

"Get out," he demanded, completely ignoring her response.

"Hang on. If you just talk to me for a minute, explain to me what—"

"I said get out!" he yelled at the top of his lungs. "Get out! Get out! Get out!"

David suddenly began grabbing things off of the tray that sat by his bed and chucked them at her with an alarming force. She actually had to duck to avoid them, though one came dangerously close to hitting her upside the head.

At the same time, the door banged open behind her,

and several nurses rushed inside, followed by a couple of security guards she had seen earlier wandering the halls. While the nurses tried to calm David down, the security guards quickly led her from the room. Thankfully, one of them grabbed her purse for her on the way out.

Madelyn was shocked by what had just happened, shaken to her very core, and she didn't say a word as she was escorted from the building. She had no idea what had set David off like that or what she had done to deserve that kind of treatment. It was completely out of the blue, and she wondered if he maybe had some kind of head injury. How else could she explain going from hot and heavy to him throwing her out of the hospital like that while simultaneously ending things?

After saying goodbye to the security guards, she walked back to her car in a confused and somewhat angry stupor. David blaming her for what happened to him was both cruel and uncalled for. She had nothing to do with it. Nor did she know what 'psycho' he was talking about. She was frustrated and hurt by his reaction to her, along with the fact that he wouldn't stop freaking out for two minutes to explain to her what had happened and why he felt it was her fault.

As Madelyn neared her car, she pulled her cell phone out of her purse and quickly dialed her best friend's number. She needed someone to vent to, and there was only one person in the entire world she was willing to do so with.

"Hey. I thought you were going to see David today," Melanie's voice came through the phone after only two rings.

"I did," she said bitterly, digging out her keys as well. "And the asshole had me escorted out by freaking security."

"What? Why?"

"He blames me for his being in the hospital, apparently."

"That… that doesn't make any sense, Madelyn."

"You're telling me. Listen, I need to ask a favor." She paused next to her car and leaned against the door, pinching the bridge of her nose.

"Anything. What's up?" Melanie said a little too quickly.

That was how Madelyn knew Melanie felt sorry for her. It was, after all, her fault she was in this mess in the first place. She was the one who had forced Madelyn to step out of her comfort zone and give David a chance. Now, she was all too eager to offer her help when she didn't even know what the favor was. Madelyn didn't need pity, she needed answers.

She hated the fact that she was about to ask this of Melanie, but the reality was that she didn't have any other choice. David certainly wasn't going to tell her, and since Melanie was a detective with the Cedarwood Police Department, she was the only one left to ask.

"It's a big ask, Mel," she began. "It could get you into a lot of trouble. So, if you aren't comfortable with it—"

"What's the fucking favor, Madelyn?" Melanie asked firmly.

She pressed her lips together and looked around the parking structure to make sure she wasn't going to be overheard. For a brief moment, she thought she saw someone standing over by one of the concrete support pillars a couple of rows down. But she quickly brushed it off as being a trick of the light because she was clearly alone.

With a sigh of resignation, she raked her fingers through her hair. "I need you to find out what happened to

David last night. I need to know why he blames me for this."

Melanie went quiet for a few moments, and Madelyn figured she was trying to figure out the best way to decline, not that she would blame her. It was a big ask, and she could get into a lot of trouble for it. In hindsight, she should have waited until she went back to work herself since she worked at the station too. She was only a receptionist, so she didn't have the same kind of access to files that Melanie did, but she could probably figure it out. That way, it would only be her ass on the line. All of this was just going to bug the crap out of her until she knew what was going on.

"You know what? I'll do it," Melanie suddenly told her.

"Wait, really?" she asked, not bothering to hide her surprise. Even though Melanie was her best friend, she hadn't expected her to agree to something like this.

"Yeah. I want to know what his deal is too," Melanie replied. "Just give me a few days to look into it and dig up the reports and stuff."

"You are the best, Mel. Thank you."

"Awe, I love you too. Listen, I have to get back. Call me later?"

"You bet!"

Madelyn ended the call and put her cell phone back into her purse before she opened the car door. She realized then that, in her haste to get into the hospital, she must have forgotten to lock the car because it was already unlocked. Just as she was about to get in, she spotted a white envelope sitting on her seat and a hand-carved, wooden dove, both of which had her freezing in place. Maybe she hadn't forgotten to lock it after all.

Her brows creased in curiosity and confusion as she picked up the items. The little wooden dove was beautiful and carved with immensely intricate detail. She could see every single feather on the wings and tail. Whoever had carved it was clearly talented with their hands. But it was the letter that drew her attention.

The envelope was addressed to "My Little Dove," and for a moment, she wondered if it was from David. She wasn't sure how or why, but she couldn't think of anyone else it could be from. Not knowing what else to make of it, she set her purse down on the seat and opened the letter.

"Hello, Madelyn. I figured I should introduce myself, seeing as how we are going to be spending the rest of our lives together. Now, I understand that what happened to David is probably upsetting, but you will get over it, and when you do, you will realize that he was no good for you. You will forgive me too, in time, for the part I had to play. We are destined for each other after all, and I just couldn't stand watching someone else touch what's rightfully mine. You may not realize it yet, but you ARE mine. I do hope you keep that in mind because I would hate to have to hurt or kill someone else for touching you. I'll be seeing you soon. —Yours, Xavier"

Madelyn blinked at the letter a few times as a chill shivered down her spine. The hair on the back of her neck stood on end, and she suddenly felt as though someone was watching her. Perhaps what she had seen earlier was not a trick of the light after all. Her eyes darted around the garage once more, searching every corner and between every car. Every shadow she saw felt sinister and dangerous, yet, in reality, there was nothing there. At least, nothing that she could see anyway.

The letter itself was chilling in its own right. It had confirmed David's story that someone had attacked him because of her, and he threatened to do it again should anyone else touch her too. Someone clearly had her in his sights, claiming that they would be together for the rest of their lives and saying that she belonged to him.

The thought was terrifying and shook her to her very core.

Somewhere on a different level of the structure, a car door slammed shut, nearly making her jump out of her own skin. She shook herself and realized then that she was just being silly. No one was watching her. It was probably some kind of sick joke that David had concocted with his friends. It would explain why he wouldn't tell her exactly what happened the night he was attacked. He had probably wanted to end things with her and used his accident as a way to do so. Though, she still couldn't figure out why he would go to such lengths and blame her for it all. Sometimes, guys didn't make any sense to her.

After shoving the letter and the little wooden dove into her purse, she tossed it to the passenger side and climbed in behind the wheel. While the letter was creepy, the dove was adorable, and she was going to keep it. Maybe she would even put it on her desk at work. After all, it reminded her of the dove tattoo she had on her wrist, which held such a significant meaning to her.

As she drove out of the parking structure, she blasted her favorite 'girl power' playlist while also reminding herself that this was why she didn't do relationships in the first place. Men couldn't be trusted for anything more than sex, and she would do well to remember that fact, if only to avoid this shitty feeling in the future.

Madelyn brushed away the angry tears that had begun to roll down her cheeks and cranked up the volume to drown out the sound of her breaking heart. She would allow herself a little time to feel the pain the situation with David inflicted. But then, she would package it up and shove it aside just like she always did. Once again, she was going to have to rebuild the walls around her heart, and this time, she wasn't going to let them fall again. Not for anyone.

Chapter Two

Madelyn

Two days had passed since the incident with David at the hospital. The wound was still raw, but Madelyn was healing herself the best that she could. She busied herself with work and deep cleaning her house to help keep her mind off of things. The more she thought about it, the more she realized that she still didn't understand why he had treated her the way he did or why he blamed her for his attack. And that was frustrating.

Thankfully, she was meeting Melanie for lunch in a bit to go over what she had discovered in the police report David filed from that night. Hopefully, she would finally get some answers. Not that it mattered anymore as she no longer had the desire to try to clear her name with him. Not after what he did. She only wanted to know to appease her own curiosity and to see if she could figure out who it was that was stalking her.

Madelyn realized the day after she found the note in her car that it wasn't just a sick prank like she originally thought—or hoped. She had found another note on her desk when she got to work the next morning, telling her how beautiful she looked, how he hoped that she had a good day, and that he was counting down the minutes until they could be together. It wasn't as creepy as the first note had been and was kind of sweet in its own way, but it did make her wonder how the hell he got in and out of the station without being seen. The police station was supposed to be one of the safest places, wasn't it?

After finding the second note, Madelyn felt as though she were constantly being watched. It was like she could feel a pair of eyes tracking her every move at all hours of the day. It was a feeling that she just couldn't shake, one that had buried itself so deep into the pit of her stomach that she was beginning to wonder if it would ever go away. Whether she was at home, at work, out shopping, or taking a shower, she knew, without a doubt, that *he* was there, Xavier, lurking somewhere among the shadows. But what threw her for a loop, was the fact that she wasn't as afraid of this guy as she probably should have been.

She figured it was most likely due to her past. She had been through so much as a child, more than any adult she knew, and that trauma had changed her. It had messed with her brain chemistry or something. Her previous therapist had tried to explain it to her, but she never really understood. All she knew was that things didn't always affect her the way they should.

It didn't hurt that she knew how to take care of herself too, though. After everything she had been through, she had made it a point to take as many self-defense classes as possible. She had been told that it was overkill, that she would probably never need it in her lifetime, but it made her feel better all the same. It made her feel more confident and sure of herself.

Steam billowed out of the bathroom door as she

exited, a towel wrapped around her body and one in her hand as she dried her hair. She stopped short when she spotted the long purple box with a matching purple bow sitting on her freshly made bed. Not only had that box not been there twenty minutes ago when she got into the shower, but she hadn't bothered making her bed yet either. Which meant that someone had been in her room at some point in the twenty minutes she had been in the shower.

Madelyn moved toward the box tentatively, as if it were a bomb about to go off. When she reached the edge of her bed, she looked around the room and down the hall to ensure it wasn't a trap. Once she was sure that she was alone, she picked up the card that was taped to the top of the box. It was made of thick, white card stock, and the note was typed instead of written, except for the now familiar signature. The package was from Xavier. Her stalker.

So far, he hadn't left anything that would hurt her, but it was still too early to know what this guy was really capable of. After all, he had put David in the hospital just for talking to her. Who knew what he would do if he realized that she wasn't going to agree to be his as quietly as he hoped?

Dropping the towel she was using to dry her hair, she opened the card so she could see what the note said in its entirety.

"I watched you last night, and what a beautiful sight it was, watching you come on your fingers. Who were you thinking about, I wonder. I can't wait until the day that I get to feel you come around my cock because then I'll be able to die a happy man.

After looking through your room, I realized that you didn't have one of these. I thought I would give you something to help tide you over until we are together. All I ask is that you think of me when you use it. – Forever Yours, Xavier"

Madelyn pressed her lips together as she set the note down on the bed. Knowing that he had watched her masturbate the night before was unnerving, but she should have known better. The guy was everywhere, and he didn't seem to be leaving anytime soon. Unsure of what else to do, she flipped the top off the box.

The moment she moved the tissue paper, she pressed her fingers to her lips to stifle her laughter. Inside the cheerful purple box, on top of the sparkly tissue paper was the biggest vibrator she had ever seen in her life and, to top it off, it was an obnoxious neon pink color. It had to be at least thirteen to fifteen inches long and as thick as a tree branch. And it was veiny as hell too, full of bumps and ridges in all the right places. She had never seen anything like it before, and she wasn't going to deny that it looked like it could be fun. That was if it didn't tear her apart.

She should be upset with the guy for thinking he had the right to send her something like this, disgusted even. However, she wasn't. Already, she had come to accept whatever this guy decided to throw at her. Besides, what could she do? He didn't seem like the kind of guy to be easily deterred, nor did she believe he was going to stop anytime soon. Not after everything he had done thus far. The only thing she could do was let it play out the way it was supposed to. Either he'd come after her and she'd kill him in self-defense, or he'd kill her. Not much she could do about it either way.

Setting the box with the monster cock down on the floor, she kicked it under her bed. She would figure out what to do with the damn thing later. Now, she had to get ready for lunch with Melanie, and she needed to decide if she was going to tell her about her new *friend*. While she didn't trust the police—she hadn't in years—Melanie was her best friend. Her *only* friend really, and that had to count for something. At least, it should.

Madelyn had met Melanie three years ago when she first started working at the station as the receptionist. Melanie had been a patrol officer then and had taken Madelyn under her wing. Cedarwood PD was comprised of mostly men, and Melanie had said that the girls needed to stick together. She had been a big part of Madelyn's life ever since. It was something she wasn't used to, having a friend, but she was grateful for it.

The girls had arranged to meet at a little bistro down the street from the station, and a text message from Melanie told her that, as usual, she was already there and had grabbed them a table outside on the patio. It was a beautiful, sunny day, so Madelyn didn't mind. She even joked with herself that maybe she would get the chance to catch her stalker in action. Not that she knew what she would do if she did.

When Madelyn stepped out onto the patio, she spotted Melanie immediately as her bright red hair was hard to miss. She smiled to herself and made her way over toward the table. Melanie grinned at her as she approached. "Hey."

"Hey you," Madelyn replied as she sat down, hanging her purse on the chair behind her. She nodded toward the glass of iced tea sitting in front of her. "That mine?"

Melanie nodded. "Yeah, I already ordered your chicken club with avocado too."

She beamed at her friend, reaching for the glass and then taking a sip. "You know me so well," she stated, setting it back down on the table.

"Yeah, I do. And I have to be at the station in an hour." Melanie dug into her bag and pulled out a manilla folder with a case number across the top corner. "So, we need to go through this."

"Oh! Is that the report on David's attack?" Madelyn asked as she reached across the table to grab the file. She was more than a little excited to finally find out what had crawled up David's ass.

Melanie slapped her hand away before settling back in her scat and flipping the file open. However, the small smile that played across her lips didn't go unnoticed, letting Madelyn know that she was just playing around. To an extent. "Yes. It is."

Madelyn laughed and shook her head. She should have known better than to try to take one of Melanie's files in the first place. The girl had always been particular about them and was a little OCD in that regard. She was the only person in the station who didn't ask Madelyn to retrieve files for her or fix and edit reports as she preferred to do them herself. Madelyn didn't fault her for it; it was just one of her many quirks.

"According to the report, the assailant cut the power and waited for David in the basement," Melanie read from the file. "It says the guy slammed his head against the wall, dazing him. He then threatened him and punched him a couple of times before…" Madelyn watched as Melanie winced. It was odd to see her wince like that. Because she was a cop, she had seen a lot over the years, but this clearly got to her. "Before he stabbed him with a Phillips head screwdriver where the sun doesn't shine. Ouch."

Madelyn cringed herself at her friend's words, remembering exactly *where* David had been stabbed. The guy may be a jerk, but he hadn't deserved that. She wouldn't wish that on her worst enemy. It was no wonder the guy was pissed.

"David went on to say that the guy did leave him his

cell phone so that he could call for help," Melanie continued. "And, of course, he was gone before they arrived."

"Oh, how nice of him," Madelyn muttered sarcastically. That part was a little surprising though. Why would the guy risk David calling the police and identifying him? Why not just kill him? She wasn't complaining. It wasn't like she wished for David's death, she was just surprised was all.

"Right?" Melanie agreed before shaking her head and closing the file on the table in front of her. "But, I still don't see how or why David can blame you for this. Especially since he didn't even mention you in the report at all. It still doesn't make any sense. "

Madelyn chewed on her bottom lip thoughtfully. After a thorough debate with herself in the car on the drive over, she had decided that it was probably best if at least one other person knew about the fact that she had a stalker, just in case anything happened to her. However, she was still unclear as to how to bring it up.

"It makes sense if the guy was trying to get David away from me," Madelyn replied reluctantly. "If he was trying to get David to back off so he could have me all to himself."

Melanie's eyebrows raised as a look of confusion crossed her features. "What on earth would make you think that?"

With a heavy sigh, Madelyn dug into her purse. She had wanted to be sure the same guy sending her the notes was the same one who attacked David. The first note had taken credit for it, but she didn't have any proof. Even now, she didn't have any, but she did have a strong feeling deep in her gut that was telling her that it was the same person.

"I found this in my car the day I went to see David in the hospital," Madelyn explained, handing the folded piece of paper over to Melanie.

Just as Melanie took the note and began to read, the waiter came by to drop off their food. Madelyn thanked him and picked a fry off her plate before quickly popping it into her mouth. She didn't know how Melanie was going to react to this, but she had a feeling she wasn't going to be happy about it. Especially since Madelyn didn't tell her about it when she first found the note.

"Okay, why the fuck am I just now hearing about this?" Melanie asked her after a while, confirming Madelyn's suspicions that she was upset. Madelyn could see the anger and irritation on her face clear as day, her fist tightening around the letter.

She shrugged, deciding not to admit to the fact that she almost didn't tell her at all. She was trying to be better about opening up to Melanie, but she was used to dealing with things on her own. It was still a work in progress.

"I honestly thought it was a prank," she replied. "I thought maybe David had one of his friends put it there to really drive the whole thing home."

Melanie scoffed. "And now you don't think so."

It wasn't a question, but Madelyn shook her head anyway. "No, I don't. I've received a few more letters like that one along with some gifts over the last couple of days."

"What kind of gifts?"

"A couple of hand-carved wooden doves," she answered honestly, fighting a small smile at the memory of what she had found earlier. "And a monster dildo on my bed this morning."

Melanie, however, didn't find this nearly as funny as she did and raised her voice so much that it drew the attention of other patrons on the patio. "He was in your house? Madelyn!"

"Relax, Mel. It's not a big deal," she said softly, trying to defuse the situation.

Melanie's face completely deadpanned, and she looked at Madelyn as if she had lost her damn mind. "How the fuck is any of this not a big deal? This guy is stalking you."

"But he hasn't even tried to hurt me, and he's obviously had several opportunities to do so."

Madelyn wasn't sure why she was suddenly defending the guy. It was surprising even to herself. Not to mention a bit stupid. Melanie was only trying to help, trying to get more information, but she just didn't feel like this guy was a threat. At least, not to her.

"Are you forgetting that he put David in the hospital? That he nearly castrated the guy? And this right here?"—Melanie waved the note in her hand—"makes it sound like he's going to turn you into some kind of sex slave. Saying you belong to him and shit."

If she thought that note was bad, it was a good thing Madelyn didn't show her the note that she got from Xavier that morning. She would *really* lose her shit then.

Melanie shook her head. "No, I'm not going to let that happen. Let's go."

Madelyn cocked an eyebrow as she watched Melanie rise to her feet and snatch the file off the table before she shoved it into her bag. "Go where?"

"To the station. You are going to file a police report and show them these letters."

She was shaking her head before Melanie even finished speaking and folded her arms across her chest. That was completely out of the question. "No. I'm not."

"And why the hell not?" Melanie threw her arms out to her sides. "I don't get you. You work for the cops, for crying out loud. And you trust me as far as I know. Yet, you *don't* trust them? How does that even make sense?"

"My reasons are my own, Mel. Besides, I told *you,* and that's good enough for me."

Melanie growled in frustration before flopping back down into her seat and pointing her finger in Madelyn's direction. "You are such a pain in the ass. I really hope you know what you are doing because there is no guarantee that I can keep you safe on my own."

It wasn't her expectation for Melanie to keep her safe. She was confident that she could defend herself should the need arise. She just wanted someone else to know what was going on in case the worst should happen and she failed to protect herself. However, she didn't like the fact that Melanie was so upset with her. So, she decided to try a compromise. "If the guy ever makes me feel unsafe, I will go to the police, okay? Would that satisfy you?"

"No. But it's a start," Melanie retorted, picking at her salad. "You know, one of these days, you are going to tell me why you have such an aversion to the police."

"Wouldn't you rather hear more about the monster dildo he sent me this morning?" Madelyn asked playfully, hoping to lighten the mood as well as change the subject. She knew Melanie wasn't happy, but she never did stay mad at Madelyn for long.

"No! I don't want to hear about your monster cock!" Melanie snapped a little too loudly.

A group of older women who were dressed in their Sunday best and sitting just a few tables away gasped and began whispering hurriedly to one another, causing Melanie's face to flush. Madelyn laughed at the sight as she picked up half of her sandwich. Maybe, one day, she'd tell Melanie about the hell she had gone through with the police when she was a child, but today was not that day.

Chapter Three

Madelyn

Teeth digging into her bottom lip, Madelyn's eyes were wide as she watched the video that was playing on her phone. She also found herself incapable of looking away. It was wrong on so many levels, both sick and twisted, and while she couldn't believe what she was seeing, she found herself aroused by it nonetheless.

All she could do was stare at the screen as the large, tattooed hand jerked the massive and pierced cock with heavy strokes. She had never seen a cock that big before, let alone a pierced one, and she had always been a sucker for tattooed hands as well. The soft, guttural groans that emanated through the phone's speaker as he pleasured himself turned her on despite the wrongness of it all. The only thing keeping her from sliding her fingers down between her legs to relieve the growing ache was the fact that the video had come from her stalker. It was *his* cock she was looking at and being turned on by. To top it off, he was jerking off to a picture of her, one he had taken the day she had gone out to lunch with Melanie.

Over the last week, things with Xavier had escalated like something out of all the dark romance novels she liked to read so much. The primal obsession, the need and lust, the 'touch her and die' vibes he gave off. She had always wondered what it would be like to have someone feel that way about her, but now that it happened, she wasn't sure what to make of it.

Xavier had somehow gotten ahold of her cell phone number, too, and had been texting her every day since. Sometimes sweet little things like how beautiful she looked that day or that he hoped she had a good day at work. Other times, he sent some of the raunchiest and naughtiest of text messages that caused her face to heat while also needing a change of panties. He texted her as if the two of them were a couple and had been together for a while even though they had never met face to face.

Madelyn never responded, of course, the rational part of her mind knowing that doing so would only encourage him to continue or take things further. However, it was getting increasingly difficult for her to keep ignoring him. Especially when he did stuff like this.

In her messed-up mind, it had become a kind of game. The more he tried to get her attention, the more she ignored him. Push and pull. Cat and mouse. She knew she was the victim here—she wasn't stupid—but for some reason, she felt like she held all the power. It was a rather addicting and intoxicating feeling when she had spent the majority of her life feeling powerless and helpless.

"Fuck, Madelyn," Xavier groaned in the video. His voice was husky and deep as his hand pumped his shaft. "I can't wait to be inside you, baby. See how hard I am just thinking about it? About your pussy gripping and rippling around my cock as I fuck you fast and hard until you scream my name. Mmm."

Her traitorous pussy clenched in response to his dirty words, and the arousal in his voice caused a small gasp to escape her lips. He shouldn't have this kind of hold on her, and she knew that she had to be deeply broken and depraved to find enjoyment in something like this, but she couldn't help it. It was like watching a porno made specifically for her.

"I bet you feel so damn good, little dove, so tight," he continued.

Madelyn heard his sharp intake of breath as his strokes became harder and more frantic, clearly close to finding his release. It was as if he were imagining what it would actually be like to be inside of her and was getting off on it. That thought caused the ache between her own legs to intensify. She shifted on her bed, the pressure almost too much to bear, as she continued to watch the video, utterly transfixed as if it were the first cock she'd ever seen.

A few moments later, he came with a groan and her name on his lips. His cock twitched in his hand as it shot ropes and ropes of thick, heavy cum all over the picture of her. As that happened, her mind flashed with images of him cumming on her actual face, her breasts, inside of her…

Her breath caught in her throat at the sudden direction her thoughts had turned, and she quickly closed the video just as Xavier had begun to smear his cum around her face in the picture with his fingers.

Resting her head against the headboard, Madelyn ran a shaky hand through her hair. For someone who wanted so desperately to be normal, she was acting anything but. Anyone else would be terrified and would have already gone to the police. They would have then hounded the police until they did something about it. But not her. Instead, she found herself intrigued and curious. She wanted to know: Why her? What was it that caused him to fixate on her?

Her curiosity was eating away at her, and she couldn't take it anymore. She needed answers and decided then and there that enough was enough. She pulled up the text message thread with Xavier, her fingers hovering over the keyboard as she tried to figure out what it was she wanted to say. However, before she was able to even type a single word, a loud knock sounded at her front door.

The sound made her jump like a kid who had been caught with their hand in the cookie jar. She rolled her eyes at her awkwardness and set her phone down on the bed before getting up and heading down the stairs. Taking them two at a time, she skidded to a stop in front of the door and pulled it open.

A smile crept to her lips even as her brows furrowed. "Melanie?" she asked curiously, shaking her head. "What are you—what are you doing here?"

Melanie just held her gaze. "I decided that if you are not going to do anything about this freaking stalker, then I will."

Eyes narrowing, Madelyn raised an eyebrow and folded her arms across her chest.

Melanie, however, ignored her. "Now, I may not be able to do it as a cop since you refuse to file an official report. But I can definitely do it as a friend, so that's what I'm going to do. Any objections?"

"Do I even have a choice?" Madelyn retorted pointedly. Judging by the look on her friend's face, she did not.

Instead of responding, Melanie stepped around her and over the threshold, and Madelyn let her pass. Once she was inside, it was then that she realized that Melanie wasn't alone. Three men flanked her, all of them wearing gray uniforms with their names stitched over the right breast pocket and the name of a security company across the back. They were all carrying toolboxes and packages, and they smiled at her as they passed. It didn't take a genius to figure out why they were there.

Apparently, Melanie was having a security system put in. And an expensive one too, it seemed.

Deciding to leave the front door open so that the guys could go in and out as they needed to, Madelyn followed Melanie into the kitchen where she was helping herself to some of Madelyn's coffee.

The kitchen wasn't anything special, but it served its purpose. It had granite countertops and natural wood cabinets, which she felt made it feel more homey, and she recently replaced the fridge with a newer model. The coffee maker and toaster sat on the counter next to the fridge, and the stove sat directly across from the door with the microwave mounted above that.

The walls were a pale yellow, and the floor was white tile, giving the kitchen a bright and happy feel. It was something that she found to be annoying sometimes whenever she woke up cranky. Her favorite part had to be the small kitchen island, though, as one side of the island held the sink and the dishwasher while the other she had set up as a breakfast bar.

"I hope you aren't expecting me to pay for all this," she muttered as she grabbed her own mug out of the cabinet next to Melanie.

Melanie laughed and shook her head. "Oh, I know better than to expect that. Though, I'm surprised you aren't fighting me on it more."

Madelyn slid onto one of the stools at the breakfast bar, resting her elbows on the counter as she blew on the piping hot coffee. "Think of it as a compromise," she replied. "Since I won't file a police report."

"Which still doesn't make sense to me, by the way," her friend grumbled, turning and leaning up against the counter across from her.

She could see the questions swirling in Melanie's brown eyes, the desire for answers and reason. She could also see the determination, which, to her, meant that she wasn't going to let this go as easily as Madelyn had hoped. Melanie didn't like having questions without answers. She knew exactly where this conversation was heading, and she didn't like it.

"Melanie—" she began with a sigh and a shake of her head.

"Come on, Madelyn. You have to give me something," Melanie pleaded with her. "I don't like there being secrets between us."

"I'm not trying to keep secrets, Mel. It's just… it's not something I like to talk about."

She had only recently started feeling somewhat normal and believed that she and Melanie were in a good place in their friendship. If she told her the truth about her childhood, there was a very real possibility that it would change the way Melanie saw her. She didn't want that, but judging by the look in Melanie's eyes, keeping this from her was only hurting her, and Madelyn didn't want that either. She guessed there was really only one choice to make here.

With a reluctant sigh, Madelyn stared down into the depths of her coffee cup. "I told you my parents were drug addicts and that I didn't have the best upbringing," she began.

In front of her, Melanie stiffened but didn't say anything, clearly not wanting to interrupt. Madelyn was grateful because talking about her past was hard enough.

"But that's not the whole story," she continued. "I was born several months premature and addicted to drugs, along with a whole host of problems because of it. I wasn't supposed to make it, but somehow I did. My parents were both abusive and neglectful throughout my early years, and I had to learn to take care of myself at an early age. I was always hungry and always so lonely because my parents cared more about their drugs than spending time with me or putting food on the table. Then, when I was ten, they found themselves unable to pay for their habit anymore. So, they decided to sell the only thing they had worth anything." She swallowed hard. "Me."

"Oh, Madelyn," Melanie gasped.

Madelyn shook her head, cutting her off. If she didn't get this out now, she might never be able to. "It went on for years. Once they realized how much money they made from it, they brought home dozens of men every week. Sometimes multiple men a day. Some beat me, some raped me, some beat me while they raped me."

As she spoke, she could feel herself wanting to recede and hide away. She felt the nightmares of her past creeping closer and closer to her once more, making her want to curl into a ball and cry. However, she fought those urges, that fear, so that she could continue to explain the horrors of her past. For Melanie, she would do this.

"I grew up living in fear of that bedroom door opening night after night, the constant pain. I learned very quickly that I had to lock away that fear and disassociate from everything that was going on because that was the only way I was going to survive." Madelyn paused to take a sip of her coffee to wetten her now dry throat. "When I was twelve, I had finally gathered up enough courage to go to the police and tell them what was happening. To ask for help. But they, uh, they brushed me off. They didn't believe me."

"Are you kidding me?" Melanie exclaimed loudly, making Madelyn jump. However, her friend seemed oblivious to it. "They didn't do anything?"

Madelyn shook her head. "Turns out the sheriff was one of my regulars, but I guess that's living in a small town for you. And boy did he make me pay for trying to turn him in."

"So, how did you get away then?" Melanie's voice had become soft and full of pity, and Madelyn had to force herself not to cringe. She didn't want or need Melanie's pity. She was on the mend. Or, at least, she was trying to be.

"When I was fourteen, I was having some severe abdominal cramping and heavy bleeding," she explained. "My parents tried to ignore it, saying I would get better in a couple of days. They said it was just a bad period. But when it didn't ease up, my mom was forced to take me to a hospital a few towns over. When the doctor realized I was having a miscarriage at the age of fourteen, they immediately called the police. It didn't take long after that for them to figure out what was going on, and I was put in foster care."

"Damn," Melanie muttered. "I'm… I'm sorry. I don't know what else to say."

"You don't need to say anything, Mel. I've learned to live with the hand I was dealt, or at least, I'm trying to," she replied. "Unfortunately, that's not even the end of it."

Melanie's face fell, and her entire body sagged. "No."

Madelyn nodded again. "At sixteen, I was finally pulled from the group home and placed with a family. They seemed really nice, and I was looking forward to a fresh start, to maybe finally getting to experience what it felt like to be loved and cared for. Unfortunately, on my second night there, the dad came into my room, saying that he wanted to 'welcome me properly.' I went to the police the next day to tell them what he had done, but they thought I was making it up due to my past. They thought I was searching for more attention like most foster kids did, and I was forced to deal with it for two more years until I turned eighteen and could leave. I may not have been the most well-behaved kid when I went into the system, but I didn't deserve to be brushed off like that either."

Melanie sighed, her face an unreadable mask. Madelyn knew that look. She had seen it a dozen times whenever Melanie had come back from a crime scene and had witnessed something so awful that she had to hide what she was truly feeling. It hadn't been her intention to make Melanie feel that way now, but at least, now she knew the truth about why Madelyn didn't trust law enforcement.

For several moments, the two of them said nothing as Madelyn allowed her to process the horror that was her life.

"No, you didn't deserve that," Melanie finally said after a while. "And I understand now why you don't trust cops. You've been betrayed by them a lot over the years."

"It's why I'm so messed up," she added under her breath.

"Hey," she said gently, reaching across the island and covering her hand. "You are not messed up, Madelyn. You went through hell as a kid. Now, I may not be a mental health professional, but I think you are pretty damn normal, considering the trauma you went through."

Madelyn laughed softly, struggling to keep the tears burning the backs of her eyes at bay. "Things don't affect me like they should, Mel. That's not normal. That's why this stalker thing doesn't even phase me. After everything I went through, it doesn't seem nearly as bad or as dangerous." She paused and licked her lips before meeting her friend's gaze. "This isn't going to change anything, right? Between us?"

"Is *that* why you never told me this before? Because you thought it would change the way I see you?"

All Madelyn could do was shrug. It felt silly to admit it now, but that was exactly why she hadn't said anything.

Melanie smiled at her before she rounded the island. While she couldn't bring herself to look up at her friend, Melanie leaned over her back and wrapped her arms around Madelyn's neck.

"Nothing you tell me about who you are or where you came from is going to change things, Madelyn," she replied before pressing a rough kiss to Madelyn's cheek. "I know the kind of person you are now, and you are stuck with me."

Relief flooded Madelyn's body down to her very soul. It was as if she could feel the weight of that fear being lifted off of her, making her feel lightheaded. She was beyond glad that her past didn't change the way Melanie saw her; she didn't know what she would do if she lost her best and only friend.

"Oh joy," she teased, needing to lighten the mood before she burst into tears.

"Rude." Melanie playfully slapped Madelyn's shoulder before going serious once more. "And as for this stalker, I think I'm worried enough for the both of us. I've seen how these scenarios can play out."

"Relax, Mel," Madelyn told her, taking another sip of her coffee. "I hardly ever leave the house, and with this new security system in place, what more can this guy really do?"

Melanie pressed her lips together but didn't say anything more on the matter.

Chapter Four

Madelyn

Madelyn stepped out of the shower, exhausted and ready for bed. She had been busy at the station the last few days, and it was starting to get to her. She loved her job and loved being able to help people in her own way, but lately, she had been doing almost triple the workload than she had been when she first started.

The powers that be at the station had finally decided to upgrade their system, which they had been in dire need of. However, the tech who had done the job messed up somewhere along the way and ended up deleting everything. All the files, all the electronic paperwork, the whole thing. It was complete chaos as everyone had to suddenly switch back to doing things old-school. Thankfully, they had hard copies of it all for just such an occasion, but now it was her job to re-digitize everything on top of all her usual daily tasks. She had been going to work earlier and staying later because of it. The OT was nice, but it was also becoming draining.

After brushing her teeth and washing her face, she hung her hair towel on the back of the bathroom door. She secured the towel around her body as she exited the bathroom and headed into her room in search of some pajamas.

Her queen-size bed took up the majority of the room with its old-fashioned metal bed frame, complete with a metal headboard and footboard. She had been meaning to upgrade it to something more modern, but she didn't feel like it was much of a priority. Besides, she kind of liked the way the shiny silver glinted in the morning. She had it covered with a bright yellow comforter and gray sheets along with four fluffy pillows, giving the room a bright and cheerful look. It was a direct contrast to who she was as a person, but she loved the color.

White nightstands stood on either side of the bed, and a white dresser sat next to the bay window that overlooked the woods surrounding the property. In the bay window, she had a gray cushion and pale yellow throw blanket with a couple of throw pillows for when she had the time to sit there and read. The book she was currently working on sat on top of the throw blanket where she had left it the last time she had tried to read. Across from the window, she had an old wooden trunk that used to hold a TV, at least until it broke and she started using her laptop to watch her shows. The walk-in closet, the bathroom, and the door to the hallway were along the wall opposite the bed.

The room may not be anything special, but it was her favorite room in the house. It was where she felt safest and she spent most of her time when she was home. She was looking forward to finishing all the extra stuff at work so that she could start doing that again.

Yawning, Madelyn pulled a clean pair of underwear out of the dresser along with a sleep shirt and a pair of shorts. She had just set them both on top of the dresser so that she could get dressed when she suddenly heard the floor creak behind her. At the same time, the hair on the back of her neck stood on end, and she was overwhelmed by the feeling of someone else being in the room with her. The clothes she had in her hands dropped to the ground as she spun around, and that was when she saw him, standing just inside the bedroom door.

He was tall, taller than her door frame, which meant he must have had to duck to avoid hitting his head. He had a thick, muscular build hidden beneath baggy jeans and a dark, navy blue hoodie. His hands were balled into fists at his sides, the tops of which were covered with intricate tattoos. She recognized those tattoos, too, from the video she had received months ago and had saved to her phone because she was obviously demented. Her eyes widened in realization as she looked up at the face of her stalker for the first time, but the majority of it was shrouded by the hood he had pulled up over his head.

A heartbeat passed before he rushed her, and she attempted to leap over the bed to get away, but he was much faster than she was. His massive arms circled her middle, pinning her arms at her sides as she crashed back against his solid chest. The air whooshed from her lungs and her heart thudded a frantic beat as she struggled against his grasp, but he was far stronger than she was.

His hot breath tickled her ear as he chuckled. "Did you really think that fancy new security system would keep me away, little dove?"

In that moment, Madelyn wanted to slap herself because she *had* believed it would keep him away. While he continued to text her, she hadn't found any more gifts or notes in the house since Melanie had it installed, so she had thought that was the end of it. Clearly, she had been wrong, and she was furious with herself for getting complacent.

Xavier leaned down and ran his nose along the column of her neck like he was smelling her and trying to memorize her scent. It sent chills down her spine and managed to knock her out of her shocked and fearful stupor. What was she doing? She wasn't a helpless little girl anymore. She had prepared for this.

As hard as she could, Madelyn stomped on his foot. It didn't do as much as she hoped because he was wearing boots, but it did cause him to lift his head. The moment he did, she struck. She threw her head back, slamming it into his face. She had been aiming for his nose, but because he was so tall, she only managed to hit his mouth, and she felt his teeth dig into her skull. It still had the desired effect though as he ended up releasing her in surprise.

Madelyn didn't look back as she bolted out of the room. Her only thought was to get away and keep the towel wrapped tightly around her body. She wished she had her cell phone so that she could at least call Melanie or maybe even the actual police this time, but since she didn't have that, her only option was to get out to the street and then run to a neighbor's house. Surely, he wouldn't come after her if she wasn't alone.

She was only a foot away from the stairs, and that much closer to freedom, when Xavier managed to catch up to her. He snagged her around her waist again, causing her to scream, and then slammed her against the wall, knocking the wind out of her once more. She fought against his grasp and somehow managed to get a hand free, which she used to punch him in the side of the face.

His head snapped to the side, but it didn't seem to hurt him as much as it did her.

It felt as though she had punched a brick wall even though she knew she had used the correct form. She had practiced her punches countless times, but it seemed as though his jaw had been made out of concrete.

Before she knew what was happening, Xavier had her wrists pinned to the wall above her head with one massive hand, and all she could do was silently pray that the towel shielding her nakedness didn't fall as he grinned at her, his blood staining his teeth from the cut on his lips. The blood was from either her headbutt or her punch, she didn't know which.

"Well, that was fun," he breathed, his body pressing against hers so hard she could feel his erection pressing against her belly. "Little dove's got some bite to her."

"Let me go, and I'll show you just how much bite I have," she spat bitterly. He laughed but didn't let her go, making her growl in frustration. "What do you want, Xavier?"

It was something that she had been wanting to know the answer to ever since she found the first note. It was driving her crazy, trying to figure out what this guy wanted from her, and since she was incapable of getting away from him, she wasn't about to pass up the opportunity to find out. That was, of course, if he would even tell her.

He lifted his free hand and brushed those tattooed knuckles down her cheek. She flinched away from him but only because it was the right thing to do, not because she felt she needed to. Which was strange.

Even now, in her precarious situation, she didn't feel like she was in any danger. If anything, she felt safe, secure, and that really threw her for a loop.

His fingers continued their gentle caress down the side

of her neck to her bare shoulder. "You already know what I want. We are meant to be together, you and I."

"Bull," she hissed back at him, not knowing where this boldness came from. Here she was, face to face with her stalker, and she was provoking him. She had to have a death wish or something. "You don't even know me. You can't possibly know that we are supposed to be together."

"I can, and I do," he retorted, his eyes following the path of his fingers from beneath his hood. "And I know more about you than you think."

His fingers traced a lazy path from her shoulder to her collarbone, and her chest was rising and falling with her rapid breathing as goosebumps erupted in the wake of his fingers. The fact that he felt like he had every right to touch her was unnerving, as was the fact that her body found it rather pleasant.

He pulled his bottom lip in between his teeth before continuing. "I know about your parents, Madelyn, and I know what they did to you. I know about your foster father too. I know you haven't had any lasting relationship apart from Melanie and that you work at the police station as a receptionist. Your favorite color is yellow, your favorite animal is a platypus, and when you are concentrating really hard on something, you get this adorable little crinkle right between your eyebrows." He smiled, lifting his eyes to hers. "See, I know you?"

"H-how?" She gasped, her voice finally breaking. "How do you know all that?"

His fingers teased the top of the towel. "I'm good at what I do. I've been waiting for this, you know. The chance to meet you face-to-face. I know you feel it, Madelyn. This pull between us, the connection. It's fate. And we both know, you can't fight fate."

There was no way she was going to give him the satisfaction of knowing he was right. It made no sense to her at all, but even with him breaking in, pinning her against the wall, preventing her from leaving, and touching her as if he had every right to do so, she still didn't feel threatened. She was angry and pissed off, sure, but she didn't feel like she was in danger at all. She wouldn't go so far as to say she trusted him, nor would she say that it was some kind of pull or connection, but something was going on. It was just something that she hadn't figured out yet.

She lifted her chin to meet his eyes, which she now realized were a beautiful ice-blue color. "If you are so convinced that this is fate, then why not approach me like a normal person and ask me out? Why follow me? Why stick to the shadows?"

He chuckled, his breath caressing her face. "Because one—I'm anything but normal, sweetheart. And two—you aren't quite ready to know the truth about what I am, about what you are to me."

Her breath hitched when his finger dipped in between her breasts. She hated the way her body reacted to his touch and the fact that it clouded her mind so easily. If she were anyone else, she would be fighting him and trying to get away, not carrying on a conversation like they were old friends. So, why wasn't her body getting the message?

"W-what does that even mean?" she asked, the question coming out far more breathy and aroused-sounding than angry and firm as she had intended.

"Don't worry, little dove. You'll find out soon enough."

Madelyn shook her head, trying to clear her mind, and let out a nervous laugh. "You're crazy," she told him bluntly. Though, in all honesty, she didn't think 'crazy' was a strong enough word. Delusional, completely unhinged, or maybe even psychotic would be a better fit.

"Don't I know it," he agreed with a laugh. "Though, a lifetime of being alone will do that to a person."

Xavier released her wrists but didn't step away. Instead, he placed one hand on either side of her head. If she wanted to, she could easily kick him in the balls and take off, and she had been planning on doing just that. However, the words that came out of his mouth next made her pause.

"We are a lot alike in that regard, you know. My father was abusive too, and he made me watch as he killed my mother. That happened when I was eleven, and I've been pretty much on my own ever since."

Madelyn tried to ignore it, she really did, but hearing that small tidbit about his past touched something deep inside of her. His words managed to reach the small, terrified little girl she had been all those years ago, and her heart squeezed in her chest. Eleven years old. That was a very young age to find yourself all alone, and she knew exactly how that felt. She had been through that and so much more. The fact that they had something in common was not what she had expected.

Instead of responding though, Madelyn pressed her lips together and swallowed. That commonality aside, she didn't want to engage him any further. Who knew what kind of damage she had already done by engaging this much?

The two of them stood in the hallway in a tense silence. While Madelyn was uncomfortable and unsure, Xavier seemed to be perfectly happy standing there as his eyes roamed over every inch of her. She had never felt as exposed or vulnerable as she did in that moment. Even when she told Melanie about her past, it hadn't been as revealing as this.

As he toyed with the edge of the towel again, she

squeezed her eyes closed and rested her head against the wall. That was too much, too far, and she didn't think she could bear it. "Please, don't."

"Relax," he murmured. "We aren't doing anything tonight. Even if you are looking mighty delicious. I just wanted us to have this little introduction. I wanted you to be able to put a face to the man you are going to spend the rest of your life with." He pressed a gentle kiss to the side of her neck, right over her rapid pulse, and then another to her cheek before finally taking a step away from her. "Get some sleep. We will talk again soon."

When she felt him leave, her eyes snapped open, and she watched as he descended the stairs and headed right out the front door. Just before he closed it, he looked up at her and winked. Then he was gone.

Madelyn let out a breath and slid to the ground, her back still pressed against the wall. All at once, her body began trembling as she tried to figure out what just happened. She was so angry that she hadn't fought back more, that she hadn't told him to leave her alone. Instead of doing either of those things, she had just stood there like a scared rabbit. What good were the self-defense classes if she didn't use what she learned against an actual attacker?

Chapter Five

Xavier

Xavier: Now that we finally met face-to-face, when are you going to let me take you out?

Madelyn: Who says I'm going to go out with you? Just because you say we are 'destined' to be together doesn't make it true. You are just some creep who follows me around. Which you should probably stop doing, by the way, before I go to the police.

Xavier smirked at his phone as the waitress stopped by with his lunch. He was sitting at the bistro across from the station, the same one that Madelyn liked to frequent on her lunches. He didn't need to look at the tracking device he had planted on her car to know where she was at this exact moment because he knew her work schedule by heart. The station's electronic security was a joke, and he had been able to gain access within a matter of minutes.

Usually, he would watch her throughout the day through the security cameras, but today, he wanted to be near her. Or at least as close as he could be without being detected. Having been so close to her, close enough to touch her, as he had been able to do a couple of nights ago, it hadn't been enough. It would never be enough.

He nodded once at the waitress without looking up from his phone as he typed back a response. They were making some real progress now that they got their first meeting out of the way. She never used to respond to him before, but over the last couple of days, she had been. Granted, she had mainly been telling him to leave her alone, sometimes going so far as to tell him to jump off a bridge, but he knew deep down she didn't mean it. She was just confused and in denial about what she felt for him, which was normal, considering the circumstances.

Xavier: Sweetheart, if you were going to go to the police, you would have done so already. I think you are just afraid of what you feel for me.

Madelyn: The only thing I feel for you is hatred and loathing.

Xavier: Liar.

. . .

He knew all about her past. He knew of her intimacy and trust issues too. That was why he was taking things slower with her than he wanted to. But the monster inside of him was beginning to get impatient. He wanted to have his mate by his side already, was desperate for it, which was why he was pushing things a little harder now.

Madelyn: *I'm not a liar!*

Xavier: *Really? So you hate and loathe me so much that you watch the video I sent you of me stroking my cock while you play with yourself? How many times HAVE you gotten off to it now?*

Madelyn: *How the hell do you even know that?*

Xavier: *I told you, I'm always watching, little dove. You could have my cock, you know. All you have to do is ask, and it's yours.*

Madelyn: *Fucking creep!*

Chuckling, Xavier picked up his sandwich and took a bite. He could picture her getting flustered, the color rising to her cheeks and neck as she struggled to maintain her composure while at work. He had seen how his dirty words affected her, and now he used them to mess with her. It was the only bright spot in his otherwise tragic and boring life.

Xavier: You love it. You like knowing that I'm always watching you. You get off on the attention.

Madelyn: I do not! Go away!

Xavier: Keep telling yourself that, sweetheart. I'll have you begging for my cock soon enough.

Because he had been so caught up in their banter, he hadn't realized anyone had sat down at his table until they cleared their throat.

Xavier's eyes shot up and away from his phone, his body tensing as he grabbed the knife from the table, instantly going on the defensive. At the same time, he silently cursed himself for letting his guard down. He knew better than that.

"You're getting sloppy in your old age, Xavier," the familiar, husky voice of his old partner, Isabelle, said pointedly.

Once he realized there was no threat to be found, his tension eased, and he set the knife back down on the table before leaning back in his chair. He smiled at the beautiful redhead before responding. "What are you doing here, Isa?"

After the death of his parents, Isabelle's father had taken him in, and the two of them had been raised in a life that was surrounded by violence and murderers. Like him, Isabelle had become a lethal weapon herself, and they had teamed up more than a few times over the years. Through those years, they had become close before he had up and left that life behind him.

She was still as beautiful as he remembered too. Bright red hair, pale skin, piercing hazel eyes, and a killer body to boot. However, she didn't hold a candle to Madelyn's beauty, he realized now.

Isabelle's lips quirked up slightly. "What, I can't just drop in and check on you from time to time?"

"That would require you to have an iota of empathy, which we both know you do not possess."

She rolled her eyes in response. "Alright, fine," she grumbled, reaching forward and taking a fry off of his plate. To anyone else, they would appear to be just two old friends enjoying some lunch together. The other patrons in the bistro had no idea that they were in the presence of two of the most merciless killers in the world.

"My father sent me. Wanted me to let you know that Colby marked you and plans on taking you out," she added once she finished chewing.

Xavier chuckled and shook his head. Colby was his self-proclaimed nemesis. The guy was jealous of him and the fact that he had always been favored by Rodrigo.

Rodrigo was the one who found him and saved him from himself. Xavier had just killed his father for murdering his mother, leading him to become a rogue shifter at just eleven years old. He had become self-destructive, volatile, and had *wanted* to die. He had just been too much of a coward to do it himself.

Rodrigo gave him a purpose, an outlet for the insatiable blood-lust that came with being a rogue. He had raised him and given him the family he never had. Because of that, Xavier busted his ass to become one of the best. He always did what he was told and always took the more complicated jobs, which allowed him to climb the ranks within the family quickly. He couldn't count the number of times he had been chosen for a job over Colby, and he had always known the guy held a grudge. He just didn't know that he would go so far as to mark him as a target, especially since he was out now and no longer a threat.

Marking was how Rodrigo dealt with discord in the family. They were able to mark one of their own that they had a problem with, essentially challenging them to fight to the death. However, if they didn't follow through and kill their mark, then they forfeited their own lives instead, as payment for wasting the family's time. It was harsh, brutal, but that was why marking was not taken lightly.

"I'm not worried about Colby," he replied easily. "The guy has never been able to best me."

"I don't know, Xavier," Isabelle retorted. "He's gotten stronger and more volatile since you left. He's downright psychotic now."

"Well, then. I bet that makes *you* happy. You little freak," he teased her.

Isabelle was one of the select few in the 'family' who knew what he was and hadn't been afraid of him. In fact, seeing him shift and kill had been a major turn-on for her as she had ended up in his bed more than a few times after missions. She had told him that there was something about watching him lose control and rip a man to pieces that did it for her. The way he went feral and completely lost it, especially when he had been covered in blood. There were no feelings behind it, of course. It was just sex for the sake of getting off, and he had enjoyed it for a time. But that time had long since passed.

Isabelle scoffed. "Please. I wouldn't touch that diseased

pencil dick if my life depended on it." She leaned forward in her chair after a glance behind her and lowered her voice. "Look, just don't underestimate him, okay? He plays dirty and breaks the rules more often than not anymore. The only reason my dad keeps him around is because he knows too much. Besides, I was able to approach you all too easily when I wasn't even trying to be inconspicuous."

He shrugged again as if he were brushing off her critique, but she was right. He had been distracted as of late, but that was what happened when a shifter found their mate. Their mate changed them, and he had already felt himself changing over the last few days. Madelyn made him want to be a better man, a man who deserved her. While he didn't think that was entirely possible, he owed it to her to at least try.

The fact that he was so distracted and the fact that he had changed since Isabelle had known him wasn't going to change. He was still going to pursue Madelyn until she agreed to be his. He was just going to have to make sure he kept his guard up at all times.

"I appreciate the heads up, Isa," he told her honestly.

"Of course."

Xavier expected her to get up and leave now that she had done what she came here to do as she wasn't usually one for idle chit-chat. However, she remained in her seat, staring out of the window. He had seen that look on her face more than a few times, and he knew what it meant. There was something else she needed to tell him.

"What is it?" he pressed.

She looked back at him and folded her arms across her chest. "We want you to come back, Xavier. My father wants you to come home."

"He's the one that granted my freedom in the first place," he reminded her.

"I know, but he regrets it. You were like a son to him. Besides, if you came back and rejoined the family, Colby wouldn't stand a chance."

"He doesn't stand a chance now," he said, shaking his head. "I'm enjoying my freedom, Isabelle. You can tell Rodrigo that I appreciate the offer, but I'm not coming back."

Even if he had wanted to, he couldn't see himself rejoining that life. Not now that he had Madelyn. There was no way she would approve of that lifestyle, and she deserved better than a life of violence and murder.

He was lucky Rodrigo had let him go in the first place as that was usually unheard of. Once someone was a part of the family, they had to get permission to leave, and that rarely ever happened due to the sensitivity of what they did.

"Then do it for me!" Isabelle suddenly blurted, causing him to blink in surprise.

He sighed and leaned toward her over the table. "Isabelle—" he began.

"We had fun, didn't we? Killing and fucking our way around the world. We were unstoppable. Powerful. And we had more money than we needed. Don't you miss that?"

"Sometimes," he admitted truthfully. "But I have too much blood on my hands now, and my soul is blacker than black. I needed to get out before I went completely feral."

That was why he decided to leave in the first place. He had nearly lost himself to the beast inside. The killing no longer satiated the bloodlust, he spent more time as a wolf than in human form, and he had nearly killed an innocent. That was never the kind of man he wanted to be, and he knew then that it was time to leave that life behind. He was grateful that Rodrigo allowed it because he had every intention of killing anyone who stood in his way of leaving, and that probably would have been what sent him over the edge entirely. Even if Madelyn hadn't been in the picture, he wouldn't risk going back to that dark place.

"I guess I can understand that," Isabelle muttered, running her fingers through her hair. "Things just haven't been the same since you left."

"Aw, you miss me," he teased.

"Ass." Color flooded her cheeks. She had always hated being called out on her emotions, especially when she was so damn adamant that she didn't possess any. He used to be the same way. At least, until Madelyn. Even so, he would say that Isabelle was the closest thing he had to a friend because the two of them were messed up in ways that no one else could really understand.

With their line of work, it wasn't easy or smart to get close to anyone, not that he had ever wanted to before. Those kinds of ties gave their enemies and rivals a weakness to exploit.

"So, what's next for you?" he asked, picking up his sandwich again and taking another bite.

Isabelle shook her head. "I don't know. I'm in between assignments right now. What about you? What are you doing with your overabundance of free time?"

He shrugged. "Nothing. And that's the beauty of it. I can do what I want when I want."

"Not to mention *who* you want," she added with a wink.

He nodded. "That too."

"*Is* there someone you're fucking these days? Someone special maybe?"

"Nah, no one special." The lie came quickly and easily. He may be close with Isabelle, but she was still a stone-cold killer, just like he was. He knew better than to trust her to know about Madelyn.

"Well, that's lame. I was hoping to live vicariously through you! I'm not getting any either, you know."

The implication was clear in her voice, but he wasn't falling for it. Not this time. He didn't want or need to sleep with Isabelle now that he had Madelyn. They may not be to that point in their relationship yet, but they would be soon. He was getting to her, and now they were even talking. It wouldn't be long before he had all of her. The beast wouldn't hold out forever.

When he didn't respond, Isabelle sighed before rising to her feet. "Alright. I gotta jet. Don't be a stranger, alright? Just because you are out doesn't mean you get to pretend that we don't exist."

"I'll keep that in mind. It was good to see you, Isa."

Isabelle nodded before walking away. It *had* been nice to see her again. He meant it when he said he sometimes missed what his life had been before, and she had been a big part of that. They had given him purpose when he had needed it the most. Now, though, he had a whole new purpose. A purpose that included the beautiful brunette with a penchant for telling him to go to hell. There was no reason for him to cling to that old life, not when he was trying to forge a new one with her.

Thinking about Madelyn had him picking up his phone from where he'd placed it on the table, screen down, while talking to Isabelle. He smiled when he realized he had another text from her.

*M*adelyn: *Keep dreaming, asshole. I won't be begging you for shit.*

. . .

Xavier: You say that now, but you'll cave. Eventually.

Madelyn: You sound so damn sure of yourself.

Xavier: Because I am, little dove. We are end game.

Madelyn: NEVER. GOING. TO. HAPPEN.

Xavier smirked to himself as he tossed some cash onto the table and left the bistro. They would see about that.

Chapter Six

Madelyn

The cool night air bit into her exposed skin as Madelyn stepped out of the station. It had been another long and tiring work day, and there was a new bottle of wine at home that was calling her name. As she made her way down the block toward the parking structure, she pulled her keys and her cell phone out of her purse, turning the phone back on. She'd had to turn it off earlier in the day to be able to get some work done because Xavier would not stop texting her, and it was distracting.

As she made her way down the block, toward the public parking structure where all civilians were required to park, her mind drifted back to the man that she couldn't seem to stop thinking about. She knew that she never should have responded to him, but after their little confrontation back at her place, she couldn't help it. There was something about him and his obvious obsession with her that she found interesting as much as she did irritating, and now he was all she could think about.

She had begun to hate how much she enjoyed their banter and despised the fact that she didn't like it whenever he went quiet because she didn't know what he was doing. She tried telling herself it was because she was worried about what his next move would be, but even she knew that was a lie. While she may not know where the situation was going to go, she was determined to find out.

If Melanie ever found out what she was doing, that she was responding to her stalker when she had insisted that she continue to ignore him, there would be hell to pay. Melanie would be pissed that Madelyn was encouraging him, but she was a grown-ass woman and could make her own decisions. And if one of those decisions was to engage in social sparring with her stalker, then so be it. At least, that's what she kept telling herself.

As usual, once she arrived at the structure, there were only a couple of cars left on the first few levels. Because the several blocks around the station were under construction, the only other people who parked in the structure anymore were construction workers. Despite her recent change in hours, they both arrived and left before she did, so parking was a nightmare in the morning. Today, she had to park up on the sixth floor, and of course, the elevator was broken. Taking the stairs up six flights wasn't the best feeling after such a long day.

After what seemed like forever, she finally made it to the sixth floor and stepped out of the stairwell. Her quick footsteps echoed loudly on the slick concrete as she crossed the lot toward her car, and a couple of the lights flickered overhead. The place was always eerie and gave her a creepy vibe.

Once she reached her car, she opened the door and

tossed her phone and purse onto the passenger seat. She was just about to climb in behind the wheel herself when she heard the sound of rapid footsteps behind her. Rolling her eyes, she spun around, half expecting to see Xavier sneaking up on her, and was fully prepared to give him a piece of her mind. However, she found herself staring down the barrel of a gun instead, and Xavier was *not* the one on the other end of it.

The man who had snuck up on her was tall and skinny with shaggy brown hair that appeared as though he hadn't showered in a while. He had a brown, scraggly beard and an unkempt mustache, and his clothes were filthy and rumpled. His dirty gray jacket had several holes in it as well. If she didn't know any better, she'd think he was homeless, but his actions, his shiftiness, suggested that he was probably a junkie in withdrawal. Which made him even more dangerous.

"One wrong move, bitch, and I blow your fucking head off," he told her, his voice nasally and grating.

Most people would be terrified in this situation. Madelyn, however, had to resist the urge to sigh. She just couldn't seem to catch a break. First, it was Xavier and his stalking; now, it was this asshole. When were these people going to learn that she wasn't as easy a target as she looked? Not to mention how stupid it was for him to be trying to do this so close to the station.

"Alright," she said softly, lifting her hands in front of her while being careful not to make any sudden moves. She didn't need to freak him out and risk him shooting her before she could come up with a plan. "What is it that you want? Money?"

"Nah, gimme the keys," he replied, nodding toward the car as he shifted on the balls of his feet.

Madelyn held the keys to her car out, dangling them by

a finger, making it appear as though she were complying with his demand. When he lunged for them, she flinched, and the keys dropped to the floor between them, which was all part of her hastily made plan. As she expected, the man paused only for a moment before he bent over to pick them up. That was when she struck.

Grabbing the back of his head, Madelyn slammed his face into her knee as hard as she could, his nose shattering on impact. He gripped his nose with one hand as he stumbled back but lifted the gun in the other. All of her self-defense training instincts kicked into high gear, and she didn't even think about it before she rushed forward and grabbed his forearm, shoving him against the pillar next to her car. She banged his wrist against the concrete over and over again until he lost his grip and the gun clattered to the ground.

She knew that she needed to keep the weapon away from him if she had any chance of surviving this encounter. So, she kicked it with the side of her foot while still struggling to keep her would-be attacker pinned. By some miracle, the gun sailed off the side of the structure and into the dark, which eliminated that threat at least. But her luck had seemingly run out by that point.

Because she had been so distracted with trying to get rid of the gun, she had unknowingly loosened her hold enough for the man to yank his arm free. He twisted around and took hold of her hair, using her own momentum against her to slam her head against the same concrete pillar she had attempted to break his wrist on just moments before.

"You stupid bitch!" he sneered at her, pulling her hair so hard several strands were ripped out of her head. She winced as stars began to invade her vision. "All you had to do was give me the fucking car. Now I'm gonna kill you!"

When he yanked her backward, she stumbled as blood dripped into her eyes. The pain was expanding through her body, making it so that she couldn't stop him from landing a heavy blow to her ribs. She cried out as the air was forced from her lungs. Thankfully though, she managed to block out the pain long enough to be able to stop the punch he tried to land to her face before she grabbed his arms and thrust her knee into his crotch. While he was doubled over, she spun around and began moving in the direction of the stairs, knowing now that she needed to get away. It was clear that, even in his current state, he was stronger than she was. There was no way she could win this.

Madelyn's steps were clumsy, her head pounding so hard that it was blurring her vision. The blows had disoriented her, made her dizzy, and that made walking a bit of a struggle. Unfortunately, she didn't get more than five feet before the junkie was on her again, tackling her to the ground with the force of a linebacker. Rolling her onto her back, he circled her neck with his hands, cutting off her air.

His grip on her throat tightened, and Madelyn realized that all that time and money sunk into self-defense classes had gone to waste. No matter what she did, this guy seemed to get the upper hand, and it had been the same way with Xavier too. She clawed and scratched at his hands, but nothing seemed to work, and he was squeezing her neck so hard that her vision was already beginning to tunnel.

The pressure on her throat trapped the blood in her face, making her already throbbing head feel like it was going to pop right off of her shoulders. The pain was debilitating, consuming every rational thought she had until only one thought remained: She was going to die.

Her life was going to end at the hands of some brazen junkie who was dumb enough to try to carjack her a block away from the station, and there was nothing she could do about it. She had put up a good fight, but it just wasn't good enough. *She* wasn't good enough.

Determined not to go down without at least getting a few more shots in, Madelyn used what little strength she had left to yank hard on his forearms while simultaneously bucking her hips. The junkie flipped over her head and landed hard on his back.

With her airway now unobstructed, Madelyn coughed and sputtered as her lungs sucked in the oxygen she so desperately needed, and she managed to roll onto her stomach. Her arms shook as she pushed herself up onto her knees to face her attacker again. Much to her dismay, he was already rising to his feet and had pulled out a knife. Even though he was swaying and bloody, he *still* had the upper hand.

Her shoulders sagged with defeat as she lowered her head toward the ground, accepting her fate. She was just too tired and weak. There was nothing left in her to fight him anymore, no matter how much she wished she could. She had let her guard down, and now she was going to pay for that.

A low, deep growl suddenly filled the space around them, and she looked up just in time to see Xavier tackle the man from the side. He was again in the same hoodie he had been wearing the other night, which was how she knew it was him, but to her, he looked like a white knight coming to her rescue in her time of need. A small spark of hope ignited in her chest. Maybe she wasn't about to die after all.

Both Xavier and her attacker went down in a heap of limbs just a foot away. When Xavier rose onto his knees, the hood fell off his head as he lifted his arm and slammed his fist into the junkie's face over and over again. But the sound of bones and cartilage cracking beneath the blows was completely overshadowed by the sight before her. Not only was Xavier losing it on the guy, but his eyes were also *glowing.*

Madelyn blinked, rooted to the spot and wondering just how hard she had hit her head. Surely, she wasn't seeing what she thought she was seeing. It was impossible. Eyes weren't supposed to glow like that. It just wasn't normal. People weren't supposed to have elongated canines or claws for hands either, though, and Xavier did. Why? How?

Lost in her own mind, she hadn't realized that the junkie had stopped moving until Xavier lifted his head back toward the ceiling and roared. She flinched at the completely inhuman sound as she had never heard anything like it before. But before she could even process that, along with his current appearance, her eyes widened as he suddenly lurched forward and ripped the junkie's throat out with his teeth as if he were some kind of feral beast with a taste for blood.

A warm spray of fresh arterial blood splattered her face, neck, and chest, but still, she didn't move. She didn't think she could. All of her instincts were screaming at her to run, but she knew better than to run from a predator, and that was exactly what Xavier was right now. A predator. The question was: Who was his prey? Her or the man he just killed who was lying in a growing pool of his own blood?

A cold chill ran down her spine, and bile rose in the back of her throat as Madelyn had never seen a dead body before. She had never had to watch the life drain from a person's eyes. The guy deserved it, of course, but being a witness to death up close and personal was not something she had ever prepared herself for. None of this was.

Xavier spat blood and bits of flesh from his mouth and onto the floor before he grabbed the guy's jaw in his clawed hand. "No one fucks with what's mine," he growled in his face even though the guy was dead and couldn't hear him.

All she could do was watch with both fear and trepidation as Xavier closed his eyes for several moments, taking deep, shaky breaths, before he rose to his feet. She flinched again as he turned and closed the distance between the two of them in a few strides. Her reaction didn't seem to bother him though as he crouched down in front of her and gently tilted her chin up with bloody knuckles. "You alright, little dove?" he asked, his voice low.

Madelyn blinked, and his eyes were normal again, but they were full of both concern and residual rage. The claws had vanished, and his teeth were back to regular size too. Seconds ticked by as she wondered if she had imagined it all. The only indication that she had seen what she did was the blood that coated his front, starting at his lips and going down to the waistband of his jeans.

The thought of what he had done had her eyes instinctively flicking over to the growing puddle of blood and the dead body just a foot away. Her stomach rolled at the sight. The guy's neck was gone, just a hollowed-out hole where his throat used to be. The skin was jagged and torn, and she could see the ripped ligaments, tendons, and even a bit of his spinal cord. She whimpered and swallowed the bile that began to rise in her throat again as Xavier tugged on her chin, forcing her to look at him again.

"Don't look at him; look at me," he told her. "Focus on me."

"You… you killed him."

She had to be going into shock. Her mind was blank as if someone had hit the delete button on everything but what had just occurred. It was replaying over and over again in her head like a horror movie on repeat. She found herself emotionally numb too, a blank void where nothing was registering. Once the shock wore off though, she knew that she would break; there was no doubt about that. It was just a matter of time.

"I did," Xavier replied as he began examining her wounds. The gentleness of his touch was a contradiction to the viciousness in which he had just attacked that guy. She didn't think he was capable of being gentle after that. "And I'd do it again. No one touches what's mine." His eyes met hers and blazed brightly for a moment, making her blink again. "And you are mine, Madelyn. Whether you want to admit it or not."

Because she didn't have the mental capacity to fight him right then, she just averted her gaze, biting her lip. She instantly regretted that though as she got a taste of the man's blood that now splattered her own body.

Xavier yanked his sweatshirt off and wrapped it around her shoulders. She hadn't realized that she was trembling until he began rubbing her arms through the material as if trying to warm her up. "You are in shock," he pointed out. "But I don't think you have a concussion. Your pupils look normal."

"I… I think he broke my ribs," she muttered, unsure of why that mattered. It was just all she could think of to say.

"Here, let me see." Xavier helped lift her to her feet, one hand grasping her arm and the other on her waist. Dizziness washed over her once she was upright, but he kept a hold on her until she was steady.

Grabbing the hem of her shirt, she gently lifted it, wincing as she did. Xavier pressed against her side in multiple places, some of them causing her to hiss through her teeth. When he was done, she lowered her shirt and instinctively grabbed onto his biceps. After what just happened, she needed the comfort his touch seemed to bring.

"They're not broken. Just bruised," he explained.

She looked up into his pretty blue eyes, her vision only slightly blurry now. "How did you know I was in trouble?"

"I watched you come into the structure and realized you were taking longer than normal to leave," he said with a shrug. "You sure you're okay?"

"I… I think so. Th-thank you."

Not once in her life did she expect that she would be thanking her stalker. It felt strange and unnatural, and she was sure she would end up regretting it later when she was thinking clearly again. But, whether she wanted to admit it or not, he *did* just save her life, and that warranted her gratitude.

Xavier cupped her cheek with his hand, and for the first time, she didn't shy away from him. "You never have to thank me, little dove. I will always protect you. I'm just sorry that I didn't get here sooner." He bent down a bit and pressed a kiss to her forehead. "But right now, you need to get out of here. Go home and get cleaned up. I'll handle this."

Madelyn shook her head, not understanding. "Xavier, I can't leave the scene of a crime. I have to stay. I have to give my statement to the police."

"And what exactly are you going to tell them, Madelyn? How are you going to explain this?" he asked, cocking an eyebrow at her as he motioned toward the body.

"I…" She paused, trying to rationalize what she had witnessed, but she was coming up blank.

The truth was she didn't know how she would explain

it because she didn't know how to rationalize what she saw. Then, there was the very real possibility of the cops thinking *she* was the crazy one. If the police didn't believe her when she tried to tell them about her parents and her foster father, there was no way they would believe her when she told them that Xavier had glowing eyes, claws, and extended canines. That just screamed 'crazy', even to her.

"I don't know."

"Exactly. No police. I'll handle this. Just go get cleaned up."

Without waiting for a response, Xavier helped her back toward her car, stopping briefly to pick up her car keys, which were still lying on the concrete where she had dropped them. Then, he assisted her in getting into the front seat. She looked over at him as he placed the keys into her hand, and she realized that it didn't feel right to just leave him behind. He had protected her, saved her. If he got caught trying to clean up her mess...

"Go," he told her as if he could read her mind. "I'll be fine."

After giving him a small nod, Xavier closed her door, and she struggled to put the key into the ignition, her hands still shaking violently. Once the car was started, she pulled out of the spot and headed toward the exit, watching Xavier disappear in the rearview as she did. Something had changed between the two of them that night; she could feel it as if it had left a mark on her. Something was different, and she wasn't sure if that was a good or a bad thing.

Somewhere along the way home, the adrenaline began to wear off, and Madelyn had to pull over to the side of the road because she began crying so hard that she could no longer see through the windshield. Her mind was a mess, her body was sticky with drying blood, her head was killing her, and all she could do was replay the events of the attack over and over again. And every time she went through it, she came to the same impossible conclusion: Xavier wasn't human. And she had no idea what she was supposed to do with that information.

Chapter Seven

Xavier

Xavier dressed as quickly as possible, having not even taken the time to fully dry off after his shower. The fear and uncertainty he saw in Madelyn's eyes when she looked at him after he had killed that man bothered him, though he wasn't sure why. He was used to people looking at him like that, mainly right before he killed them. However, he didn't like the fact that his actions had done that to her, and his wolf was anxious to make sure that she was okay. After yanking on his boots, he snatched up a clean t-shirt, not bothering to put it on right away, as he stormed out the door.

It had taken him longer than he would have liked to move the body of Madelyn's attacker into the trunk of his car, clean up the blood, and destroy all traces of them from the structure. It was almost midnight by the time he had finished, and he had debated on just going right to her place without cleaning himself off because he needed to see her that badly. Eventually, though, he decided against it as he didn't want to risk making things worse for her by showing up still covered in blood. The relationship between them was tentative as it was.

This was not how he had expected the night to go at all. He had planned on making sure Madelyn got home okay after work and then playing with her a bit more. It had become a game, a routine, one that he had grown rather fond of and knew she had too, even if she still wouldn't admit it. He wanted to feed off that, wanted to cultivate and grow it until the bond between them was unshakable and she wouldn't be able to deny it anymore. Instead, the night had taken a dark and fatal turn, and he may have shattered every bit of progress they had made by giving her a glimpse of the monster he struggled with daily. He just hadn't been able to help it.

When he had seen that man's hands on her and realized that he was planning on killing her, his already fragile restraint had snapped in an instant. His only thought was to save her, to protect his mate, and he ended up killing the man in a fit of blind rage. He had torn the guy's throat out with his teeth, right in front of her. Then, instead of reporting it like she had wanted to, he made her leave and cleaned up the mess himself, essentially making her an accessory to murder. That hadn't been his intention, but it had been drilled into him to avoid the police as much as possible.

Ultimately, he was not doing a very good job when it came to convincing her that they belonged together, which was why he needed to check on her now. Not only did he need to make sure she was okay, but he needed the chance to explain.

Xavier had made it to Madelyn's place in record time and, thankfully, without incident. It was a good thing, too, because the body in the trunk wouldn't look very good if he had been pulled over. The plan was to get rid of it *after* checking on Madelyn because he knew where his priorities were. He wasn't worried about blood or the smell because he had wrapped it in plastic sheeting, which he still conveniently had in his trunk.

Climbing out of the car, he let himself into her house with the key he had recently acquired. He then punched in the code to the alarm to disarm it and took a moment to listen to the sounds of the house. The washer was going in the laundry room, and Madelyn seemed to be upstairs in her bedroom. After everything that happened, and due to how late it was, he had expected her to be asleep by now. Instead, it sounded as though she were pacing and muttering to herself. It was a good thing he was there because he knew how to calm her down.

Taking the stairs two at a time, he headed in the direction of her bedroom. Because he had been there more than a few times over the last few weeks, he knew the place like the back of his hand. He spotted her the moment he stepped into the room and felt some of the tension leave his body like a physical weight had been lifted. Her hair was wet from the shower she had taken, and her skin was pink as if she had rubbed it raw, trying to rid herself of all the blood. The bloody clothes she had been wearing were gone now too and had been replaced by a baggy sweatshirt and sweats.

He always did prefer her like this; dressed comfortably and with no makeup. It showed who she *really* was, the face behind the mask, so to speak. However, the sight of the bruises beginning to form on her face and neck, along with the deep and jagged cut on her forehead, was like being doused in a bucket of ice water.

His jaw clenched as he took a moment to try to reign in

his residual anger. It wasn't her fault she was attacked, but if she hadn't been so hell-bent on pushing him away, he could have prevented all of this.

"Madelyn," he said softly. She spun on him, her eyes wide, but he continued to move toward her. "You okay?"

"No," Madelyn laughed, though the sound was devoid of any humor at all. "I… I watched you kill a man, Xavier. You ripped his throat out with your fucking teeth! And your eyes…"

"I'm not going to apologize for what I did if that's what you're after," he replied by way of response. "Because, as I told you, I would do it all over again."

Madelyn scoffed. "Do you even care that you took a life?"

"No," he stated with no hesitation. "He hurt you. And I've killed people for a lot less than that."

The answer didn't require much thought on his part because, in his mind, there had been no other decision to make. It wasn't the first life he had taken, not by a long shot, and he doubted it would be his last. When it came down to a choice between her and anyone else, she was the one he was always going to choose. He would burn the whole fucking world down if it would keep her safe.

"Goddamn it, Xavier! I don't belong to you!"

Her words reignited his fury and angered the beast inside of him. He still hadn't regained complete control of his monster after letting him free earlier, and he growled as he suddenly snatched a handful of her hair. Not hard enough to hurt her, just enough to pull her to him and lift her gaze to his own.

"You can say that as many times as you want if it will make you feel better," he told her, his voice low and strained as she struggled against him. "But that doesn't make it true. You *are* mine, little dove. I have already proven that I will kill to protect you, and you'd best believe that I would die to protect you too. I knew it from the moment I laid eyes on you. I know I don't deserve you. I'm not a good man by any means. I've killed more people than I can count and tortured even more than that. My soul, and my heart, are black, and I am so far beyond broken that it makes what I did tonight look like child's play. And yet, Fate still brought me you. You may not believe me right now, but you will eventually. I'm not going anywhere, Madelyn, so get fucking used to it."

For several moments, the two of them stood in the middle of Madelyn's room, just glaring at each other. His shoulders heaved with every breath, and the muscles in his jaw ticked as he ground his teeth together. He was fighting like hell to regain some sense of himself again after his admission. This was the turning point in the relationship between the two of them, and arguing was not going to solve anything, nor was it going to help the situation. Madelyn wasn't in her right mind at the moment, and she needed him to be her rock, even if she refused to say so.

All of a sudden, her palm collided with the side of his face, the slap echoing through the room as the sting blossomed across his cheek. But then, before he could register what had happened, her lips crashed against his, and her hands gripped the front of his shirt, holding him to her.

For the first time in a very long time, Xavier had been taken by surprise. With as often and as hard as she fought the bond between them, he hadn't expected her to be the one to make the first move. He figured it was probably her conflicting emotions, along with the shock and adrenaline, that was screwing with her rational thinking. It was preventing her from being able to fight the bond between them, and the only thing her mind was telling her to do was to give in to it. And he was inclined to let her.

If he were a good man, he would stop this, if only to keep her from regretting it later. But he had already stated that he wasn't a good man, and his wolf was tired of being denied. Once they did this, there was no going back, and that was exactly what he wanted.

A smirk spread across his lips at the thought as his fingers tightened in the strands of her hair. His cock throbbed painfully and hardened beneath the constricting material of his jeans as he pulled her flush against his body.

He teased the seam of her lips with his tongue until she opened for him, and then his tongue dove into her mouth as if of its own accord. Out of all the women he'd been with before, none of them had felt as heavenly as this. It was better than anything he could have ever possibly imagined, and he had only kissed her.

The kiss deepened, becoming more frantic and demanding. Though, whether it was on her part or his, he didn't know. Nor did he care.

Nipping at her bottom lip with his sharp teeth, eliciting a gasp from Madelyn, he released her hair and then literally tore the sweatshirt from her body, hating how many layers stood between them. He hadn't realized that she wasn't wearing a shirt underneath it though, which meant that she was now bare to him from the waist up. Whatever control he thought he had regained was gone just as quickly. There was no way this was going to be anything but hard and rough, but it was clear that was what they both needed.

Without giving her a chance to react, he dipped his head and took one dusky pink nipple into his mouth while pinching and rolling the other between his fingers. Madelyn moaned, her back arching, as her fingers dove into his hair. When he flicked his tongue against the tight peak, her nails scraped against his scalp. The fact that she was so receptive to him only further solidified that they were meant to be.

While this was far more than he had expected to happen when he came to check on her, he needed more. He needed to be closer to her, to feel her. All of her. He needed to bury himself so deep inside of her that she forgot every horrid thing that happened tonight.

Gripping her ass in the palms of his hands, he lifted her off the floor. Her legs wrapped around his hips as he carried her to the bed and laid her on it. As he righted himself, he hooked his fingers into the waistband of her sweats and yanked them off before pulling his own shirt over his head. He tossed them both to the ground somewhere over by the closet.

Madelyn took in the sight that was his chest and abs before he settled himself in between her legs, using his broad shoulders to push her thighs apart. His gaze never left hers as he licked along her pussy, the taste of her exploding on his tongue and making him groan. She was already drenched for him, and he had just gotten started. Her eyes fluttered as her head flopped back onto the pillows, and he smirked before doing it again.

No matter how many times she tried to push him away, she wanted this. She wanted him just as much as he wanted her. He knew that for a fact now, and that knowledge spurred him into action as he went to town.

Sucking her clit into his mouth, he pushed a finger inside of her at the same time. Madelyn moaned, and her hips left the mattress. He placed his free hand on her lower abdomen to hold her down, flicking his tongue relentlessly against the small bundle of nerves while simultaneously adding a second finger. She was tighter than he realized she would be, which meant that he was going to have to stretch her out a bit if she had any chance of taking his cock. While he enjoyed a bit of pain, he didn't want to break her.

"Oh, fuck," Madelyn moaned, her back arching as she tweaked her nipples between her own fingers. "Harder, Xavier."

Xavier groaned, his dick throbbing so hard it felt like it was going to explode. Her pussy began to clench around his fingers, and he knew that she was already close. He moved his fingers faster, harder, knowing exactly what spots he needed to hit to bring her to the release she so desperately craved. His tongue continued its assault on her clit, alternating between flicking and sucking, as her moans increased and her legs began to shake. Just before her orgasm crested, he nipped at her clit with his teeth.

Madelyn screamed as she came, her pussy clenching tightly around his fingers as he continued to thrust them into her, helping her to ride it out. He watched with rapt attention as her body writhed on the bed, and he loved every second of it. He loved knowing that he was the one that made her feel that good.

Without slowing his fingers, he sat back on his knees and unbuckled his pants with his free hand. If he didn't get inside of her soon, he was going to lose it.

When he finally freed himself, he removed his fingers, making Madelyn whimper. She went to instinctively close her legs, but he pried them back open and settled his hips between them. He kissed her, the head of his pierced cock lining up with her perfectly. Madelyn bit his lip hard, making him growl as he lifted his head to meet her eyes. She licked her lips and gave him a single nod, which was all the confirmation he needed. Her hands gripped his shoulders as he slammed into her in a single thrust.

Madelyn let out a strangled cry, her nails piercing his

skin at the sudden invasion. He had felt the stretch and resistance as he entered her, and he tried to blink away the stars that had dotted his vision. She was so tight, so warm, and so wet that he almost came right then and there. It didn't matter how vivid his imagination had been when he jacked off, thinking of Madelyn, over the last couple of weeks. Nothing compared to the real thing, and he knew then that he would never get enough of her.

Without giving her any time to adjust, he pulled his hips back and slammed into her again and again, setting a rough and demanding pace. She cried out, her nails leaving thin pink lines down his back, but she was also moving her hips in time with his and meeting him thrust for thrust. He had dreamed of this moment since the first night he saw her, and now that it was here, he couldn't control himself. Not that Madelyn seemed to be complaining.

The emotions that had accumulated from the events of the night seemed to be leading their actions, and the rougher he was with her, the more it seemed to turn her on. When he tweaked her nipple sharply, her pussy clenched around him as she bit into his shoulder. He moved his lips to the side of her neck and sucked a bit of skin into his mouth, no doubt leaving a mark, and he reveled in the way she moaned in response. The bites and scratches she was leaving on him as well were wounds that he would wear with pride. She could mark him all she wanted because he planned on doing the same soon enough.

His hips slammed into hers hard enough to bruise, and her pussy gripped his cock in all the right places. He lifted his head and looked down at where their bodies were joined, not breaking his rhythm. The sight had him growling deep in appreciation.

"Jesus, fuck," he groaned, moving his hand down between them to circle her clit with his thumb. "Look how good you take me, little dove. This pussy was made just for me, wasn't it?"

Instead of responding, Madelyn wrapped her legs around his waist, allowing him to go deeper, which he took as answer enough. He gripped her jaw with his hand and kissed her again as he picked up the pace. Her headboard banged against the wall, chipping off both paint and plaster, and the lamp on the nightstand shook violently, but he didn't care. Nothing else mattered but them and the way their bodies seemed to fit together so perfectly.

Already, he could feel the tingle at the base of his spine, the tightening of his balls as they slapped against her. His cock swelled with every thrust, but he held off the oncoming orgasm, wanting the two of them to cum together.

Xavier sat back on his legs again, one hand gripping her hip, his fingers digging into her soft and delicate flesh, while he circled her clit with the other. Her walls clenched around him tightly as her heels dug into his back.

"That's it, little dove. Cum for me," he demanded through clenched teeth, his fingers pinching her clit hard. "Cum on my cock."

Madelyn gripped the comforter, a strangled scream on her lips, as she came around him at his demand. Her walls clamped down on him like a vice grip, and after slamming into her three more times, he came with a roar. His cock pulsated with every wave of release, his whole body tense as he filled her with thick ropes of his cum. His eyes blazed, and his canines elongated in his mouth with the need to mark her, but he wasn't going to do that right now. Not yet.

After they both came down from their intense orgasms,

Xavier leaned over her and pressed his lips against hers before he rolled off of her and onto his side. Shifting the blankets on the bed to cover them both, he gathered her into his arms and tucked her head beneath his chin.

He smiled to himself as he stared up at the ceiling. He had been wrong when he had assumed that what happened earlier tonight had damaged the progress they had made. The fact that she had let him fuck her had proven that. While he wanted to stay the night, he knew she wouldn't like that come morning. So, he would stay until she fell asleep, and that would have to be enough. She was going to need time to reflect on what they did tonight, and he would give her that because it wouldn't be long now before she gave in to him completely.

Chapter Eight

Madelyn

The next morning, Madelyn was once again pacing her bedroom floor, her hair wet from her recent shower. She was dressed in her bathrobe and had her cell phone clutched in her hand as she tried to psych herself up enough to make the phone call.

There was no way she could go to work today because she was still too shaken up. She just wasn't sure if it was because she had watched Xavier kill someone to save her, because of the words he had said to her afterward, or because she'd had sex with him.

When she woke up that morning, she found herself sore in various places, and not just because of the attack. Her head still throbbed, and the bruises on her face and neck were more prominent now, but what she had been more concerned about was the soreness between her legs and the copious amounts of dried cum on her thighs. The memories of the three times Xavier had railed her before finally taking his leave had plagued her thoughts ever since she woke up. It was all she could think about, and she hated it.

He had not been gentle with her at all, not that she had expected him to be. It had been rough, demanding, just like he was, and yet, she had loved every bit of it. She had never cum so hard or so many times before, and the third time around, *she* had been the one to initiate it. It was the best sex she had ever had, and when she went in to take a shower that morning, she realized that she was also covered in hickeys. There were at least eight on her neck and another six on her chest as if he were trying to lay claim to her.

It was as if Xavier was more attuned to her body and what she needed than she was. He knew all the right spots to hit and the perfect amount of pain to add to her plea-sure. In the past, she had always tried to keep her enjoy-ment of pain hidden because she didn't want people to think she was a freak, especially after everything she went through as a child, but Xavier somehow knew all about it, and he seemed to enjoy it just as much as she did. It was just wrong on so many levels.

She had no idea what had gotten into her or what had made her lose control of herself that way. The more she thought about it though, the more she blamed it on her near-death experience. It was the only explanation she had. Her body had been going into shock, running solely on adrenaline. It messed with her rational thinking and made her want to find comfort and solace in another person. Xavier just happened to be there at the time.

With a mental shake, Madelyn quickly dialed Melanie's number. She needed to get this over with so that she could start processing what she had done, but she hated lying to her best friend. She had been doing that a lot lately, and it made her feel dirty. Melanie had always been there for her, and keeping her in the dark about this stuff made her feel like she was being a crappy friend.

"Hey," Melanie answered. "Shouldn't you be on your way already? You better not be calling me while driving. That's illegal you know."

Madelyn cleared her throat. "I know, and I'm not. I'm actually calling to let you know that I won't be in today. Maybe not even the next couple of days. I think I… p-picked up some kind of cold or flu."

The emotional crack in her voice helped to sell the lie a little too easily.

"Oh no! That sucks," Melanie replied. "Are you okay? Do you need anything? You never get sick, so I don't really know what to do here."

"You don't need to do anything, Mel. I'm fine. It's nothing a little rest won't fix."

Though that was probably the biggest lie of them all. There was no way a bit of rest was going to fix whatever was so broken inside of her that it prompted her to sleep with the man who had been stalking her. The same man she had watched kill a guy and whom she believed was not even remotely human.

She was still kicking herself for not asking him about that fun little tidbit too. At the time, she had wanted to believe that it was the hit she took to the head that made her see what she thought she had, but she had seen his glowing eyes and elongated canines again the night before, every time he climaxed. She had spent a good chunk of her time in the shower, trying to figure out what the hell he could possibly be, but she was still coming up blank.

"Alright. Well, I'll let the captain know what's going on," Melanie said, pulling her out of her mind and back into the present. "You feel better, and call me if you need anything, okay?"

"Thanks. Will do."

Madelyn hung up her phone and headed to her dresser.

Once she was dressed and feeling more like a person, a dirty, lying person but a person nonetheless, she made her way down the stairs to make some coffee. Once she had some caffeine in her, she would be more likely to come up with an explanation for what she had seen since that was the thing that was bothering her the most. Not that he had killed a guy in front of her, not that she had fled the crime scene, making her an accomplice, and not even the fact that she slept with him. What was bugging her was not knowing exactly *what* he was.

As it were, her mind was coming up with some of the weirdest things to try to rationalize it: alien, cybernetic robot, science experiment gone wrong.

She laughed softly at the ridiculousness of her own mind, but that was all she could come up with. Everything else was just too far-fetched or downright impossible.

Sipping on her coffee, she contemplated just messaging Xavier and demanding the truth. She had a right to know who she was sleeping with. But *was* she sleeping with him though? Had their weird and twisted relationship gotten to that point, or was it only a one-time thing that happened after a traumatic event?

The guy was dangerous, deranged, and he had been stalking her for crying out loud. Wanting him was wrong and stupid, and it made her just as crazy as he was. Even if the sex was absolutely incredible and she *did* feel drawn to him. Though, she'd never admit that to him. His ego was large enough as it was, as were some other notable parts of his body.

Her pussy throbbed at the memory, bringing with it the pleasant sting that she had woken up with that morning. He had been larger than he appeared in the video he sent her, and the thought of it made her want him all over again. She wanted to feel that stretch of him entering her roughly, the way his piercing hit all the right spots, and she wanted to feel his hand around her throat again.

Madelyn slammed her coffee cup down on the counter, silencing those thoughts. What the hell was wrong with her?

Sighing heavily, she pinched the bridge of her nose when she heard a knock at the door. She ground her teeth together in irritation, figuring that it was Xavier coming back after fucking her into oblivion and then leaving her last night. She couldn't seem to get a moment's peace anymore, but at least, he was knocking this time. She really needed to figure out how he was getting around the security system and the locks. There was too much about him that she just didn't know, and that bugged her way more than it should. Maybe today would be the day that she finally demanded some answers.

She moved through the kitchen and into the foyer where she disarmed the alarm. Once that was done, she unlocked the door and pulled it open, a snarky remark already prepared. However, it wasn't Xavier standing on her porch as she had expected. That seemed to be happening a lot lately. She had gotten so used to him being everywhere that she was starting to expect it.

Blinking, she took in the man in front of her. He was wearing a crisp, navy blue suit and had dark blond hair with striking hazel eyes. His skin was tan as if he spent a lot of time in the sun, and he had thin lips, a strong jaw, and a crooked nose that appeared to have been broken and set wrong. He was muscular too, but more so like a surfer and less like an MMA fighter like Xavier was.

"Ms. Hart?" he asked, giving her a dazzling smile.

"Yeah," she replied hesitantly. "Can I help you?"

Her first thought was that he was a salesman of some kind. But they didn't usually know people by name. Maybe he was a lawyer or with the nearby church or something. Either way, whatever he was selling, she wasn't interested.

"I'm actually hoping we can help each other." He reached into his coat pocket and pulled out a badge. "I'm Special Agent Colby Marks with the FBI."

With her stomach churning dangerously, her mind began to go to all the worst possible scenarios. Maybe Xavier didn't hide the body of the man he killed for her as well as he thought he did. Or maybe they had been seen on a security camera somewhere. She knew the structure didn't have any, none that worked anyway, but there could have been some around the area that she didn't know about. Then again, why would the FBI be involved in the murder of a junkie instead of the local police? It seemed a bit extreme.

Forcing herself to relax and to stop jumping to conclusions, she met the man's eyes and gave him a small smile. "What can I do for you, Agent Marks?"

"If you have a minute, I'd like to talk to you about a man named Xavier St. James," he told her simply.

Madelyn swallowed hard, the coffee she drank turning sour in her belly as she shook her head. "I'm sorry, I don't know who—"

"Ms. Hart, we've been tracking Mr. St. James for years now, and we have access to his recent phone records. I know you know who I'm talking about."

Shifting nervously on the balls of her feet, she reluctantly stepped aside, allowing him into the house. He nodded his thanks as he crossed the threshold into the foyer. Once she closed the door, she began leading him into the living room so that he could say whatever it was he needed to say. If nothing else came of this meeting, at least, she now knew Xavier's last name. That was one thing she hadn't known about him yet, one question answered.

After taking a seat on the couch, she motioned for him to take the chair across from her. "I'm not sure how much help I'll be," she admitted, leaning back against the cushions and crossing her legs to appear comfortable. "I don't know him that well."

Agent Marks cocked an eyebrow. "Do you make it a habit to sleep with guys you don't know?"

She bristled at his remark, her guard beginning to rise. She didn't trust the FBI any more than she trusted the police, and she didn't like the way he was already speaking to her. It felt like he was implying that she was some kind of hussy. Who she slept with and how well she knew them beforehand was none of his concern.

"Excuse me?"

"As I said, I've been tracking him for quite some time." He must have seen the look on her face because he quickly continued. "Don't be embarrassed. *A lot* of women find themselves incapable of resisting his charms. However, lately, his sole focus seems to be on you. Why do you think that is?"

Madelyn wasn't even going to try to figure out how he knew that Xavier was focused on her or how he knew they had slept together. But the way he was talking made it sound like he believed the two of them were in a relationship instead of the fact that Xavier was stalking her. Though, after last night, she didn't know where they stood anymore.

"I assure you I have no idea," she replied truthfully through clenched teeth.

If Agent Marks noticed how irritated she was becoming with him and the conversation, he didn't let on. "Ms. Hart, I feel like I should warn you about the kind of guy you are getting into bed with."

"I really don't see how that's any of your business," she snapped.

She didn't like how this interaction was going at all. It seemed very unprofessional and felt more like the guy was here on some kind of personal vendetta. It was in the way he spoke to her and the tone of his voice. Why else would he bring up the other women Xavier had been with and attempt to 'warn' her about him? There was no way it was solely out of the goodness of his heart. There was malice and contempt there; she just didn't know why.

"Were you aware that he was a hired gun for the Cortez Family?" he asked her pointedly as though he hadn't heard her.

Despite it being damn near impossible, Madelyn forced her face to remain impassive as she said nothing. Meanwhile, her heart began to race in her chest, and her mouth had suddenly gone dry. She had known that he had killed before last night; he had admitted as much to her. But she had no idea he had been a hitman, of all things. Though she guessed it made sense.

From what she knew, which wasn't much at all, hitmen were required to learn everything they could about their target. Xavier may not have been trying to kill her, but he had done his research on her as well. He knew things about her that not many people did.

Madelyn had also never heard of the 'Cortez' family, but she figured they had to be some kind of crime family.

She made a mental note to do some googling later, once she got rid of the good agent.

"Rodrigo, the head of the family, took Xavier in after he had killed his father at the age of eleven," Marks continued to explain. "Because Xavier didn't have anyone else, Rodrigo raised him himself as if he were his own son, but he raised him to be a weapon. Though, that didn't take much considering he was already messed up and had killed his own father." He shook his head as if in disgust. "For years, Xavier dutifully followed Rodrigo, killing whoever he was told to without question or hesitation, and quickly climbed the ranks. He was paid handsomely for it too, including Rodrigo's daughter. Our sources say that they were inseparable, and everyone thought the two of them would marry. But then, eight months ago, he just up and left the family, breaking Rodrigo's daughter's heart."

"Maybe he was just tired of being used," she quipped, unsure of what else to say.

She was struggling to process this information while also trying to determine how much of it was true. While she had wanted answers, and it *seemed* like she was finally getting some, she didn't like what she was hearing. Then again, all of it was contingent on whether or not this guy could be believed. She wasn't so sure of that anymore.

He laughed, actually laughed at her comment. "My dear, Xavier wasn't being used. He enjoyed the killing; he enjoyed inflicting pain. He lived for it, in fact." He looked at her pointedly, a smirk playing across his lips. "I really hope you aren't expecting him to fall in love with you or anything because he's a monster and incapable of feeling things like love or empathy. He's incapable of anything but pain and torment, and he would destroy an innocent girl such as yourself."

"Is there a reason you came by to talk to me?" she

asked him. She was getting tired of whatever game he was playing here. He didn't know the first thing about her or what she had been through. She didn't want or need him to try to protect her if that was even what he was doing. It seemed as though he was just here to try to drive a wedge between her and Xavier.

Whatever was going on was between him and Xavier. She wanted no part in it whatsoever.

Agent Marks opened his mouth as if he were about to respond, but the front door suddenly flew open so hard it banged into the wall. Madelyn screamed in surprise, jumping to her feet as Xavier stormed around the corner. His eyes narrowed at Agent Marks, and his hands balled into fists at his sides.

The traitorous butterflies in her stomach went wild at the sight of him. He was wearing a tight black T-shirt and jeans with his signature boots. His hair was tousled, and even with the frown marring his features, he was like a walking wet dream. And he was *pissed*. However, it was clear that it wasn't directed at her as his eyes were locked on Agent Marks.

"Well-well-well. Look what the cat dragged in," Marks chided, rising to his feet. "Long time no see, Xavier."

Xavier closed the distance between him and the agent in just a few strides before he slammed his fist against the side of his face. "You have a problem with me, you come after me. Leave her the fuck out of it!" he roared.

"Xavier!" Madelyn squealed, rushing forward and grabbing his arm before he could hit him again and get them both into even more trouble. "You can't just go around punching federal agents! What's wrong with you?"

"Federal Agent?" Xavier sneered, not taking his eyes off Marks. "That's a new low, even for you."

Marks laughed and spat a glob of blood and spit onto her floor. "It worked, didn't it? It got me in the door."

"Wait," Madelyn stated bluntly. "You're not with the FBI?"

"Not even close," Marks replied. "I had to get you to trust me somehow. Tell me something, Xavier. I'm curious. Is her pussy better than Isabelle's?"

This time, Madelyn didn't try to stop him and even took a step back as Xavier took another swing at the guy. The sound of flesh striking flesh filled the room as Marks' head snapped to the side, but she didn't feel the least bit sorry for him.

She should have known he wasn't a real agent. She should have listened to her instincts when she started getting a bad feeling about him. If the FBI did know all that stuff about Xavier, and if it was even true, then he would have been in prison a long time ago. Which begged the question: Who was he really, and what did he want with her?

Chapter Nine

Xavier

Xavier had known that Colby was after him, thanks to Isabelle's warning a couple of days ago, but his involving Madelyn was crossing the line, and he wasn't going to stand for it. The moment he realized that Colby was inside, he lost it. He didn't even bother trying to figure out what was going on before he stormed through the door as if he had every right to be there.

In his mind, he did. The house belonged to his mate, and his mate belonged to him. The fact that Colby had dared to approach his mate meant he may as well have signed his own death certificate. The guy was lucky he had only hit him when he really wanted to tear him limb from limb.

Colby laughed and spat more blood from his mouth while Xavier flexed his fists, readying himself to deck the guy for a third time should the need arise.

"Obviously, that's a touchy subject," Colby stated, wiping his chin.

"What are you doing here, Colby?" he growled dangerously. "Your issue is with me, not Madelyn."

"Oh, relax, Xavier. I'm not here to kill you. *Yet.* I just wanted to meet the girl who seems to have tamed the great assassin."

His jaw clenched, but he otherwise hadn't reacted. He hadn't gotten around to telling Madelyn about his past yet, at least, not much of it anyway. He had wanted her to be more comfortable with him, wanted her to be more accepting. But judging by her lack of reaction behind him, Colby had already told her and probably gave more detail than was necessary.

Xavier watched as Colby scanned Madelyn's body slowly, his eyes darkening as he pulled his bottom lip in between his teeth. The guy was a sleazeball and wasn't even trying to hide the fact that he was checking her out. And right in front of him, no less.

"I can definitely see the appeal," Colby commented before focusing on Madelyn. "You know, sweetheart, I can take care of you too. Once this asshole's out of the picture, of course. I think we can have a lot of fun together."

"Fuck you," Madelyn sneered at the same time Xavier growled in warning.

Madelyn was braver than he gave her credit for. She had to know that Colby was a killer just like he was, and she still had the balls to speak to him that way.

"Oh, I'd love to. Just give me a time and a place," Colby said with a smirk, blowing a kiss in her direction.

"Yeah, that's never going to happen," Madelyn spat.

Colby shrugged in response, the determination in his eyes only pissing off Xavier's wolf that much more. "We will see about that."

"That's your problem," Xavier stated, taking a step back so that he was closer to his mate and in between her and Colby. He wanted to keep Colby's attention on him and not on Madelyn. She wasn't supposed to be a part of this. "You always seem to want what you can't have."

"That's just it though! I can have it because you aren't going to be around long enough to stop me, are you?" Colby exclaimed excitedly.

"That has yet to be determined."

Colby cocked his head to the side, ignoring his remark. "Did you even tell your little *girlfriend* that you've been marked for death?"

"No. I didn't think it was necessary. You've never been able to beat me before, Colby. I don't see how this time is going to be any different."

Madelyn's nerves were coming off of her in waves, and he felt every shift in the air when she shifted behind him. It was distracting, and the need to reassure her consumed him, but his focus was needed elsewhere. It wasn't smart to drop his guard when it came to Colby, and those instincts once again proved to be true.

"I've learned a few things in your absence though," the guy replied before suddenly pulling out a gun and pointing it at him. "Like how to lull my target into a false sense of security."

Behind him, Madelyn gasped, and he discreetly gripped her thigh with his hand, silently telling her it was okay. He wasn't even remotely surprised that Colby would try something like this. It was just like him—always quick to action and very little thought. That was why he didn't get the attention he wanted within the family. They were tired of having to constantly clean up his messes.

Xavier's job now was to figure out how to get them out of this situation with both him and Madelyn unharmed.

"Except it didn't work on me, did it?" he asked as he carefully took another step back, forcing Madelyn to do the same to put some more distance between her and the gun. "I knew you were going to try something. I am always two steps ahead of you, Colby."

"Maybe," Colby shrugged. "But that's still not going to stop me. I know you are unarmed, and if you move to try to take my gun, I'll just shoot Madelyn. Which you obviously don't want to happen either. So, you see, I win. There's no way for you to get out of this."

Triumph was evident in Colby's voice as he spoke. He really did believe that he had won; he thought he had the upper hand solely because he had gotten Madelyn involved. If anything, it had put him at even more of a disadvantage because Colby had gone after the one thing in the entire world that Xavier would give up his life for.

Colby was right about the fact that he wasn't armed. He didn't usually pack heat when he came to visit Madelyn because there was no need for it. However, that didn't mean he was completely defenseless. He had a trick up his sleeve that very few people knew about. Something that was always with him, simmering just below the surface and waiting to be set free. The question was whether or not he was ready to expose it.

Xavier had always intended to tell Madelyn the truth about what he was and introduce her to his wolf. He had just wanted to wait until she was ready to hear it. She was always going to find out about that side of him. The problem was that he wasn't sure he wanted Colby to know his secret. Who knew what he would do with that kind of information? If he revealed what he was, he was going to have to kill Colby. There was no getting around it, and that would mean another mess to clean up.

"Maybe I'll just kill Madelyn too," Colby continued

thoughtfully when no one said anything else. "That's probably the smartest idea, right? No witnesses and all that. So, I guess the real question is: Which one of you wants to die first?"

"We don't kill innocents, Colby," Xavier warned. "Those are the rules. What would Rodrigo say if he——"

"Rodrigo isn't here, is he?" Colby snapped angrily, making Madelyn jump behind him. "I marked you because I want to destroy you, Xavier. And what better way to do that than by killing the woman you so obviously love."

The air became heavy with the truth of Colby's words. His hurting Madelyn was the *best* way to destroy Xavier solely because of the fact that she was his fated mate. He *did* love her, he always had. That love may not be reciprocated yet, but it would happen over time. Of that, he was sure. He just needed to make sure they got that time.

As much as he hated to admit it, it looked as though the decision on whether or not to expose his wolf had been made for him. He couldn't let Colby hurt Madelyn, and he, himself, wasn't ready to die yet either. Not now that he had her. He wanted the chance to further explore the bond between them, the bond that had only gotten stronger since last night when he had finally buried himself inside of her.

"Madelyn," he said softly. "You are going to need to step back for me, little dove."

"What?" she whispered.

He squeezed her thigh again, never taking his eyes off Colby. "I need you to back up, baby girl. Give me some room."

Even though he could feel her confusion, Madelyn did as she was told. Usually, she fought him tooth and nail on everything, but she must have sensed the severity of the situation and decided against it. He was grateful for that because, with her out of the way, he could do what needed to be done.

She took several slow steps away from him, and he hated the distance, but it was for the best. He didn't want to risk hurting her with what he was about to do.

"Yeah, that would have been my choice too," Colby chuckled, moving to aim the gun right between his eyes. "Any last words?"

Xavier cracked his neck and then lifted his chin. "Yeah. You fucked up. You never should have come after Madelyn."

Colby's brows furrowed in confusion as Xavier made his move and lunged forward. The sudden movement startled Colby, and the gun ended up going off in his hand, the sound deafening in such a confined space to his overly sensitive ears. The bullet splintered the wall behind Madelyn, causing her to scream and drop to the floor. But at least, she was unharmed from what his quick glance in her direction could tell.

Xavier's clothes fell in tatters as he leaped over Colby's head, the material unable to fit his new form. He stretched the claws on his right paw and dragged them along the guy's cheek before he landed on all fours just behind him. Colby screamed a blood-curdling scream as blood began to pour out of the jagged wounds, and he turned his attention to Xavier, which was exactly what he had wanted. If he was focused on him, then his focus wasn't on Madelyn, and that gave her the chance to get away. Xavier stood up straight and shook out his fur before snarling and swiping his massive paw at Colby, his eyes blazing.

The acrid stench of fear filled the room, burning his nostrils, as everyone went still. Xavier chanced a look over in Madelyn's direction, to see how she was fairing with the discovery. The terror and confusion in her eyes cut him down to his very soul but also pissed him off. He had never given her any reason not to trust him, no matter how shocked she might be.

On the other hand, Colby was staring at him with wide, fearful eyes and his whole body trembling. Xavier snarled at him again and took a step forward, judging the distance between them in his head. He could be on the man in just two strides. It would be easy to take him down, and he deserved it. Not only had Colby marked him, but he had threatened Madelyn, who was innocent in all this. He had to pay for that.

However, Colby shrieked before turning and scrambling toward the front door. Xavier bounded after him, not wanting him to get away, but Madelyn's squeal of fear, as he got close to her, caused his steps to stumble, and he knew then that he couldn't kill Colby now. At least, not in front of her.

Xavier watched with disdain as Colby stumbled down the stairs. He hit the gravel face first, breaking his nose again, and his gun went flying somewhere into the grass. However, he wasted no time scrambling back to his feet and bolting toward his car, leaving his gun behind.

Colby peeled out of the driveway just as Xavier reached the bottom of the porch. He let out a roar of frustration as well as a warning. He wouldn't let Colby get away again. The next time he saw the guy, he was a dead man.

When Colby was finally gone, Xavier returned to his human form on the porch. He was naked, but he paid that no mind as he stepped into the grass and picked up Colby's discarded gun. Carrying it back into the house, he set it on the entry table before closing the door and heading back into the living room.

The moment he entered, he spotted Madelyn in the same place she was before, sitting on the floor with her knees clutched to her chest and tears rolling down her cheeks. He moved toward her. However, she flinched away from him, which stopped him in his tracks. Even after she had witnessed him kill a guy the night before, she hadn't reacted that way to him.

This was solely because she had seen his wolf, and the reaction angered the beast inside of him. He had just saved her life, again, exposing his biggest secret to protect her, and she was *still* afraid of him. All he had ever done was protect her and love her.

"W-what are you?" she stammered, slowly pushing herself to her feet and taking a step away from him.

He folded his arms across his chest if only to keep himself from reaching for her again. "I'm a shifter."

"A… a shifter?" she gasped, her eyes going wide.

He nodded once curtly.

After a moment, a strained laugh bubbled from her lips. "An assassin, a stalker, and a shifter. Jesus Christ, is there *anything* good about you?"

"Hey! I just saved your fucking life, Madelyn! Again!" he snapped at her. It wasn't intentional. He was just still struggling to calm the beast inside of him. So, his reaction was to lash out.

"And my life wouldn't have even been in danger if it weren't for you!" she screamed back at him.

Her words rang true, and he hated that, but it didn't change anything either. She was his mate. They were destined to be together. She may be struggling to accept what he was right now, but that would change. It had to. Fate wouldn't be so cruel as to pair him with someone who was incapable of accepting him.

"Were you ever going to tell me?" she asked him pointedly.

"Which part?"

"Any of it! All of it! You are the one who keeps saying that we are destined to be together. How can you even say that if you keep all this shit from me?"

"I was planning on telling you, Madelyn. But only after you accepted me, when you were ready to hear it," he admitted truthfully. "What I am is not something I can broadcast."

"Who the fuck are you to tell me when I'm ready to hear anything?" she exclaimed.

Xavier sighed and rolled his neck. Once again, arguing and screaming at one another wasn't going to get them anywhere. He needed to diffuse the situation before either one of them said something they were going to regret. Keeping all of this from her had hurt her, and he could understand that. But they needed to talk to one another, not yell, scream, or argue.

"Madelyn—" he began carefully.

"Get out," she interrupted.

He blinked. "What?"

She sneered at him, baring her teeth like a feral animal, and pointed toward the door. "Get *the fuck* out of my house."

As much as he didn't want to, he nodded, though mostly to himself. Trying to talk to her about all this wasn't going to work out the way he hoped while she was still angry and hurt. She needed time, and he had recently learned that he could be a very patient man where she was concerned. His wolf, on the other hand…

Closing the distance between them quickly, and before she could get away, he gripped the back of her neck and pulled her to him before pressing a rough kiss to her lips. "I'll be here when you need me."

"I don't need you, Xavier," she hissed.

He brushed his fingers down her cheek, wiping away some of her tears. "You do. You'll see. I'll see you soon, little dove."

With that, he turned and left the house. It looked like he was going to be driving home naked, but he had been in worse situations. Madelyn would contact him again. She couldn't stay away from him any more than he could stay away from her. In the meantime, he was going to hunt down Colby so that they could finish what they started.

Chapter Ten

Madelyn

Two days had passed since Madelyn had discovered the truth about Xavier, and she was beginning to feel like she was losing her mind. She hadn't slept, couldn't eat, and hadn't even been able to leave the house. Not because she was afraid but because she was worried that she might run into him, and she wasn't ready to face him just yet. Thankfully, she had a lot of unused vacation time saved up and had been able to make arrangements with the captain to take a couple of weeks off. She needed to get her head on straight before she could even consider going back to work. Otherwise, she wouldn't be able to get anything done.

Madelyn took another huge gulp of tequila straight from the bottle, the liquid no longer burning her throat. She had only started drinking to quiet her mind as it had been spinning out of control, and nothing else seemed to work. Now though, she was drunk and was still no closer to deciphering her conflicting emotions. So, she decided to go over what she did know.

Xavier was a shifter and could change into a wolf at will. She was angry that he had kept it from her but even more angry that she could understand why he did. If she messed up and that information fell into the wrong hands, he would end up being locked up and experimented on. Humans did stuff like that with things they didn't understand. She didn't see him being able to live a normal life at all. Instead, he would spend the rest of his days being poked, prodded, and dissected to see what made him tick, and she wouldn't wish that on anyone. On the other hand, he was also the one who believed that they were meant to be together. If that was the case, he should have trusted her enough to tell her the truth instead of her having to find out the way she did.

Truth be told, she couldn't *really* blame him for his lack of trust either though. She had been fighting this thing between them from day one. But what else did he expect her to do? Did he think he could just tell her they belonged together, without explaining how or why he believed that, and expect her to go along with it? Especially since, instead of approaching her and talking to her like a normal person, he chose to follow her, deciding to stalk her. Hell, he had mutilated the guy she had been seeing and put him in the hospital solely because they had been going out. It wasn't exactly the best first impression.

Then, there was the whole assassin or hitman thing. Though, that little tidbit didn't bother her as much as it probably should have. Everyone had a past, and that was his. The fact that his past was coming back and haunting the both of them was a bit irritating, but it wasn't an issue either. She knew, without a shadow of a doubt, that Xavier could take Colby easily. Once again, the only reason this was an issue was because he had kept it from her.

The thing that upset her the most though, what she hated to admit even to herself, was the fact that she had actually started to develop feelings for him despite everything he had done. He seemed to be the only person in the world who *truly* understood her, who knew what she wanted or needed. When he looked at her, he saw her and every broken piece of herself that she had spent years trying to hide from the rest of the world, and he didn't shy away from it. Instead, he embraced it, and that wasn't something she was used to.

Madelyn hadn't seen or heard from Xavier in two days, and she hated how much she missed him because of it. It was no one's fault but her own. She was the one who told him to get out, but now she was regretting it because she had never felt more alone than she had over the last two days.

Apart from Melanie, Madelyn didn't have anyone else she could talk to, and she couldn't exactly talk to her best friend about what was going on. Between the sex, the fact that Xavier was her stalker *and* an ex-hitman, and the fact that he was a shifter, Melanie would probably think she had completely lost her mind and have her committed. Besides, what he was wasn't her secret to tell. But all this meant that she was left struggling with it all on her own.

She glanced down at the bottle of tequila in her lap, already one-third of the way empty. Clearly, she was doing one hell of a job of trying to cope.

While Madelyn was thoroughly feeling sorry for herself, her cell phone rang on the nightstand. Her heart leaped within her chest, thinking it might be Xavier. However, one look at the caller ID told her that wasn't the case, and that tiny shred of hope deflated like a balloon.

"Hey, Mel," she answered, her words slurring slightly.

"Jesus, you sound like shit," Melanie replied. "How sick are you?"

Madelyn shook her head even though Melanie couldn't see her. "Nope. Not sick. Just drunk."

Apparently, something about that was funny because she heard Melanie laugh. "Well, that's good I guess. At least you aren't sick anymore. Any particular reason you are drinking?"

"Nope," she lied, popping the 'p'. The alcohol just seemed to make the lying easier, which she was grateful for. She didn't even have the capacity to feel bad about it right then. "Just felt like having my own party."

"Well, that's no fun, why didn't you invite me?"

Madelyn could practically see the pout on Melanie's face, and it made her smile. "I'm sorry, I thought you had work tonight."

"Well, I don't," Melanie told her. "And me and the guys were going to head over to Iggy's. Let me come pick you up. Then you can party with other people instead of all by your lonesome."

The guys Melanie was talking about were three other detectives from the station. The four of them made it a point to get together once a week to catch up and decompress away from work. Madelyn had a standing invitation, but she hardly ever took them up on it. Melanie was the only one she was close to, even if it was by choice.

If she were smart, she would turn down the offer and just stay at home. In her current state of mind, she wasn't sure she'd be much fun anyway. However, she was tired of being overwhelmed by things she couldn't explain and sick of feeling so damn sorry for herself. A night out with her best friend, where she didn't have to worry about assassins, stalkers, or shifters, could be exactly what she needed. Nothing else she tried seemed to be working.

"You know what? Yeah, come pick me up," she stated as she climbed unsteadily out of bed and stumbled her way to the closet.

"Wait, really?" Melanie asked, not bothering to hide her surprise.

"Yeah. I just need, like, fifteen minutes to get dressed and get some food in my stomach to soak up some of the alcohol I already drank."

Melanie squealed so loudly that Madelyn had to pull the phone away from her ear so that her eardrum didn't rupture as a result. She had known that Melanie would be excited; she just didn't know she would react like that. It was a bit endearing if she was being honest.

"Oh my god, this is going to be great! You *never* go out with us. The guys are going to be thrilled. Okay, I'm going to go finish getting ready, I'll see you in fifteen!"

Melanie hung up the phone before Madelyn had the chance to respond. Knowing her, she had probably done it to prevent Madelyn from changing her mind, not that she had any intention of doing so. She needed this.

The only way she was going to come to grips with everything that happened over the last few days was for her to put Xavier behind her once and for all. She didn't want or need that kind of drama in her life, and she didn't see how it would work between them anyway. They were from two very different worlds. Even if she had wanted to pursue things, it would only end in heartbreak just like everything else in her life did. There was no other way for it to go.

Even though Iggy's was a casual place, Madelyn had decided to wear her black skirt and dark blue, off-the-shoulder, long-sleeved shirt with her black ankle boots. She left her hair down but pinned up one side with a few bobby pins and put on just a touch of makeup. While she wasn't trying to impress anyone, getting dressed up a bit made her feel better than she had in days.

The act of getting ready and devouring three muffins had helped to get rid of some of the alcohol in her system as well. She was still pretty tipsy, but at least, she wasn't falling over anymore as she and Melanie made their way to the table where the guys sat. She would have to take it easy on the alcohol, but at least she was here, and she was determined to have a good time.

Lucas was Melanie's partner, so Madelyn saw him a lot. He was a tall, older gentleman with salt-and-pepper hair and a kind smile. He was married with two kids too, both of whom looked just like him.

Tristen was younger and had just made detective earlier that year, having been a beat cop at a different precinct before that. He had blond hair, blue eyes, and a smile that drove girls wild. He was also the reason that the captain was considering a 'no dating in the office' rule at the station.

Bernie was the oldest of them all and had recently moved to desk work since he only had two years before his retirement. However, he had some of the craziest stories Madelyn had ever heard about his time in the field.

All three of the men looked up as they reached the table and grinned at Madelyn.

"Well, hot damn. Look who decided to grace us with her presence," Lucas teased as they moved to sit down in their seats.

They always chose the table in the back corner because one side of the table was booth seating, so Lucas had some back support. It was also closer to the bathrooms for Bernie, who seemed to have to go every twenty minutes or so. Tristen enjoyed it because it gave him a full view of the bar and all the women.

Madelyn smiled at him and rolled her eyes as she settled into the booth beside Lucas. "Yeah, yeah, yeah. I missed you too, you ass."

"Jesus, what happened to your face?" Lucas asked her, his brows creasing once he got a good look at her.

Melanie had asked the same thing when she showed up. Madelyn had been able to cover the hickeys on her neck and the bruises from her attack with copious amounts of makeup, but there was no hiding the gash on her forehead.

"I ate shit on my way to my car," she said, telling him the same lie she had told Melanie. "You know that one area where the construction workers are always leaving things out on the sidewalk? I tripped over one of the pipes they left on the ground."

Bernie beamed at her and gave her arm a gentle squeeze from across the table as she sat down. "Only you can be that clumsy, Madelyn. It really is good to see you though. I can't remember the last time you hung out with us."

"I can!" Melanie chimed in. She hung her purse on the chair behind her and turned to face the group. "It was almost a year ago."

"There's no way it's been that long," Madelyn stated defensively. She tried to think of the last time she was here with them, but all she could remember was being here with David. Had it really been almost a year since she had gone out with them?

Lucas laughed loudly, but it blended in with the cacophony of the bar. "Geez, even I make the time to do this once a week, and I have a wife and two kids!"

"Come on, guys. Leave her alone," Tristen said simply.

"She's here now, and that's what counts. So, shall start this off with shots?"

The blond rose from his seat, a universal indication in their group that the next round was on him. She at least remembered that much from the last time she had been here with them. The others nodded their agreement.

Madelyn, however, shook her head. "I'll take a beer. I already had a third of a bottle of tequila before Melanie picked me up."

"Pregaming, nice," Tristen commented with an appreciative nod before he moved toward the bar.

Once the girls were settled and Tristen had returned with their drinks, the five of them fell into comfortable conversation. Madelyn allowed herself to get lost in the stories of what they went through out in the field, which was so much more interesting than what she did at the station. Some of the stories were so ridiculous that the four of them laughed until their sides hurt and they had tears streaming down their cheeks.

While Madelyn had debated on whether to come or not, she was ultimately glad she did. For the first time in two days, her mind was quiet and still. She found herself laughing and enjoying the conversation and companionship. It really had been exactly what she needed, and she finally felt as though she was on the right track to getting her life back together.

While Bernie went to the bathroom again and Melanie headed to the bar to grab the next round, Madelyn's phone buzzed in her purse. She pulled it out and felt the traitorous butterflies return when she saw that she had received a text from none other than Xavier himself.

Chapter Eleven

Xavier

Xavier: I am glad to see you are looking better, little dove. How are you feeling?

Madelyn's head shot up after reading the text message he sent, and she began scanning the bar, no doubt looking for him. He had done as she asked and left her alone for the last two days, but he still kept an eye on her from a distance. When he discovered that she was heading to Iggy's Bar, he decided to tag along so that he could stretch his legs. Then, when he saw her smiling and laughing with her friends, he had to reach out and see if anything had changed. It was obvious she was doing better and coping with everything she had learned, but there was the minor problem of her avoiding him that he needed to correct.

Xavier had spent the last two days in wolf form,

running and patrolling the woods that surrounded her house. Because he hadn't shifted back once during that time, he was feeling a bit more feral and wild than usual, but it was the only way he could cope with not being able to talk to her. Being away from her was torture of the worst kind and it hurt like hell. He had come to need her, crave her, and their conversations were what kept him going.

Because he had been deprived of all that over the last couple of days, it was a wonder he was able to hold it together as well as he was. Even so, he was currently warring with his wolf, the latter wanting to go over there and throw her over his shoulder like a caveman so that he could take her home and show her and everyone else who it was that she belonged to. He was currently holding the beast back, but he didn't know how long that would last.

It had been his fault that Madelyn was avoiding him; he knew that. It just didn't make it any easier to deal with.

It took her a few moments, but Madelyn's eyes finally found him in the corner booth directly across from her. He smirked at her, loving every second of seeing her beautiful eyes looking at him again. Even from where he sat, and over the noise of the bar, he heard her gasp when he winked at her.

They continued to stare at each other for several moments before her eyes narrowed at him and she began typing rapidly on her phone. A few seconds later, his vibrated in his hand.

*M*adelyn: *I thought I told you to leave me alone.*

.   .   .

He smiled at her response before typing back one of his own. As he did, he could feel her eyes on him. They were practically boring holes into the top of his head, and it made his smile grow.

Whether she wanted to admit it or not, she liked the fact that he was there. He could tell by the way her sudden arousal permeated the air of the bar, and he wondered if she was thinking about the night they slept together just like he was.

Xavier: *You did, but you didn't mean it.*

He watched as her shoulders deflated as she read his message. This time, she didn't look up at him as she typed back. Instead, her focus was solely on her phone, her tongue pinched adorably between her teeth. He had thought that she was going to try to deny it, but her response surprised him.

Madelyn: *You're right. And I hate the fact that you're right. Just like I hate the fact that I missed you these last two days, even though my feeling that way is so wrong it's not even funny.*

Madelyn: *And if you ever tell anyone I said that, I will deny, deny, deny.*

. . .

The smile he had been wearing since she locked eyes with him grew. Apparently, all he needed to do to get her to open up a bit was to supply her with a bit of alcohol. It seemed to have taken away some of her inhibitions and filters, and now she was admitting more to him than she usually would have. He wasn't going to complain though. She was only confirming what he already knew, which meant it was time to tell her what she was to him.

Xavier: There's a reason for that, you know.

Madelyn: And what reason is that, Xavier?

Xavier: It's not something that should be said through text messages. If you want to know, you are going to have to talk to me, face-to-face.

After sliding his phone into the pocket of his jeans, he folded his arms across his chest, a silent indication that he wasn't going to be talking to her through text messages anymore. The ball was in her court now. If she wanted to know the truth, if she wanted to know what he meant, then she was going to have to talk to him in person and not from across the room, behind the safety of a screen. She couldn't avoid him forever, and she seemed to realize it too if the heavy sigh and the pointed glare she gave him were anything to go by.

Xavier watched as she said something to the two detectives who remained at the table and then rose to her feet when they nodded at her before going back to their conversation. Leaving her purse in her seat and then meeting his eyes once more, she inclined her head toward the back of the bar and then made her way toward the exit, which was located over by the bathrooms. A few moments later, she disappeared into the alleyway that sat beyond the door. Xavier waited a few more moments before following.

The air outside the bar was cool and felt nice against his overheated skin. The sky was clear, and the town was quiet and calm. It was a beautiful night, even if the alley smelled like garbage, and while the setting wasn't ideal, he guessed it was better than nothing. At least she had agreed to talk to him.

Only a single light hung over the back door since it was supposed to be used as an emergency exit, which meant the rest of the alley was shrouded in darkness. Off to the right, about fifteen feet down, was the back lot. While, to the left, about thirty feet down, was the main road. Madelyn had chosen to wait for him in that direction, a few feet away, shrouded in darkness as if she didn't want to be seen with him.

Xavier joined her among the shadows, unable to keep the smile off his face as he lowered his hood. "How have you been, little dove?" he asked, lifting his hand and brushing his fingers down her cheek, loving the feel of her skin beneath his fingers again.

"Not good," she admitted as she shifted on the balls of her feet. "I'm still trying to wrap my head around it all. But I can't do this anymore. Surely, you realize how wrong this is; it's completely fucked up. I can't… I shouldn't… Dammit. I *don't* even like you."

"Well, that's a lie if I ever heard one," he muttered,

resting back against the side of the bar and propping his foot up behind him.

He took her words with a grain of salt because he knew they weren't true. She may want them to be, but they weren't. And this *did* seem to be part of the game they played, always one step forward and two steps back.

"It's not a lie!" she exclaimed defensively, putting her hands on her hips. "I don't like you."

He loved this woman with his whole heart, he really did, but she was as stubborn as a mule. She had been so traumatized by her past, so blinded by pain and heartache, that she couldn't even see what was standing right in front of her. It didn't matter how many times she denied it or how 'wrong' she thought it was, it didn't change the fact that she was his. He just needed to make her see that so they could stop with all this bullshit.

Pushing himself off the wall, he moved toward her until she was forced to take a step back. "Yes, you do. And you know how I know that?" he asked. When she only stared back at him without saying anything, he reached up and pinched a strand of her hair between his fingers. "Because you, Madelyn, are my fated mate."

The only reaction he got out of her was a slight shift and a heavy swallow. "Am I supposed to know what that means?"

"It means that my wolf recognizes you as our mate. That you are my soulmate and the one person in the entire world that I'm meant to be with. Just like I am yours. I told you, little dove, we are destined to be together. It's fate."

There it was, the plain and simple truth out in the open just like she asked. He didn't like the way it made him feel exposed and vulnerable, but legend stated that a wolf's fated mate was the one person they *could* be vulnerable with and still trust that they were safe. He guessed he was testing that theory out now.

"You can't honestly believe that's true," she said after a while. "That's… that's not possible." Her voice had lowered to barely a whisper, and he could hear her heart pattering a rapid beat within her chest. Something he said got to her or, at the very least, was *getting* to her.

He raised an eyebrow in response. "Just two days ago, you didn't think the existence of shifters was possible either. I can assure you, it's possible. And it's happened. That pull you feel? The fact that you *missed* me, even though you think you are supposed to hate me, that's the mate bond. It's trying to bring us together." He reached up and cupped the side of her neck with his hand. "It's also why I can't stay away from you, little dove. I *need* you. And I know deep down you know that you need me too."

Madelyn looked as though she were about to deny it on instinct, but she closed her mouth quickly as if she realized that she *couldn't*. It was then that an odd feeling began to spread across his chest, a warmth that he hadn't felt in a very long time. Happiness. He hadn't felt true happiness like this in years, and he wasn't quite sure what to do with the emotion.

But that was what Madelyn did to him. She made him feel things that he thought he was incapable of feeling anymore. Since he was a child, his life had been bloody and violent, and he had been trapped in the dark with no way out. He had suspected before, but now he knew that *she* was his way out.

"This is insane," she tried to say instead. "All of it. It's absolutely batshit."

"It may be insane" he replied. "But that doesn't make it any less real, Madelyn."

Her eyes bounced between his for several moments as

if trying to find any hint of dishonesty, but she wouldn't find any. It was the truth, and it was very real.

Seemingly realizing that, Madelyn gripped the front of his shirt, and her mouth crashed against his in a rough and searing kiss that stole his breath and made his dick harden in an instant. His body always did have that kind of response whenever she was around, and when her tongue teased his, he knew he had to have her right then and there.

He grinned at her as his hands went to her waist and pulled her against him, and he quickly spun the two of them around before pinning her up against the wall. Needing to feel her again, his hands began roaming her body to try to memorize her every curve.

Nipping her bottom lip with his sharp teeth, his fingers tangled in her hair before he broke the kiss. "No more back and forth, little dove," he growled, his eyes flashing. "If we do this, then we are doing this. You don't get to pull away from me again."

The sight of his glowing eyes didn't seem to bother her anymore as she lifted her chin defiantly. "I agree to give this a shot and nothing more. This doesn't mean I believe you. This just means that I'm done fighting you."

Xavier grinned, his eyes darkening. It wasn't *exactly* what he had wanted to hear, but he would take it. He knew, without a doubt, that she would accept him. Once she realized the kind of love and devotion that came along with being a shifter's mate, she would be all in. It was only a matter of time. She was his now, once and for all and it was time to make it official.

He tugged sharply on her hair, pulling her head back so that she was looking up at him. "I'll take it," he murmured. "Now, get on your knees for me. I want to see what that pretty little mouth of yours can do."

Madelyn licked her lips, and for a moment, he saw a flash of stubbornness behind her eyes, but it was gone just as quickly as it had appeared. She squeezed her thighs together and then slowly began to lower herself onto the ground as he'd told her to. Thankfully, he still had enough sense to stop her just before her knees touched the filthy concrete. He yanked his sweatshirt up over his head and handed it to her. "Here, kneel on this."

Taking the sweatshirt, she shoved it under her knees while he worked the belt and button on his jeans. Within a matter of seconds, his painfully-hard cock was freed, and she was taking him into her mouth with no hesitation while her hand stroked what she couldn't quite fit. It was heaven.

A deep groan emanated from the back of his throat as he braced himself against the side of the building with his free hand. His fingers tangled in his mate's hair as he reveled in the sight and feel of her mouth wrapped around him. If he died now, he would die a happy man because he now had everything he could ever possibly want.

Chapter Twelve

Madelyn

Madelyn wasn't thinking as she took Xavier's cock down the back of her throat far enough to make herself gag on it. Now that she knew the truth about what he was, his size made sense, and she had wanted to do this from the moment she had seen it in the video he sent her. Going down on a guy was one of her favorite things, and she wasn't about to pass up this opportunity, even if they were in an alley.

It wasn't like her to do something like this in public where anyone could walk out the back door and see what the two of them were up to, but she wasn't in control of herself. Xavier had said everything that she had ever wanted someone to say to her, everything that she had spent her whole life craving, and that struck something deep inside of her that she had thought was irreparable.

For reasons she couldn't understand, he wanted her, and, as much as she hated to admit it, he was right, and she wanted him too. It didn't seem to matter that everything inside of her said that it was wrong or that she still wasn't sure she believed in the whole 'soulmate' thing. But she had meant what she said, she was done fighting this. Whether she was really his fated mate or not, there was *something* here, and fighting it wasn't worth it anymore.

The weight of that acceptance hit her like a ton of bricks as she forced her throat to relax so that she could take him deeper.

"Fuck, Madelyn. Eyes on me, baby," he growled. Even though she hated being told what to do, she lifted her gaze to meet his and watched as his lips parted in a gasp. "That's it, just like that. I want to see your face as I fuck your throat."

The dirty words made her moan, the sound vibrating down his shaft, as she squeezed her thighs together around her wet panties. There was something about hearing him use such vulgar language that did it for her, and she wanted to return the favor.

Madelyn scraped her teeth gently along the underside of his cock, the cool metal of his piercing clicking against her teeth, and he groaned in appreciation. The sound turned her on more than any form of foreplay, and it made her feel sexy and powerful even though she was the one on her knees for him.

As she hollowed out her cheeks and increased suction, Xavier gasped, and his face tilted back toward the sky. When he looked back down at her again, his eyes were glowing brighter than she'd ever seen before, a hot sort of carnal look reflected from him.

His fingers tightened their grip on her hair, and his thrusts became frantic and punishing. Even though she braced her hands against his jean-clad thighs, he still ended up making her gag a few more times, but she didn't mind. It turned her on.

Even though her throat wanted to fight the invasion, and her eyes watered, no doubt smearing her mascara, she continued to take it. She was enjoying the fact that he was finding pleasure in her, and she had every intention of finishing him off with her mouth. Xavier seemed to have other ideas though because he suddenly yanked hard on her hair, pulling her off of him with a pop.

Her shoulders heaved as she fought to catch her breath, but she never took her eyes off him. No one had ever looked at her the way he was looking at her now, like she was the most precious thing in the world, and it made her heart squeeze in her chest. His thumb brushed against her swollen lips before dipping inside and pressing against her tongue. Closing her mouth around the digit, she gently nipped at the pad. His eyes blazed as he pulled his bottom lip in between his teeth and moved his hand to grab her jaw instead.

"Fuck. I need to be inside you. Right now." Without giving her time to respond, he pulled her to her feet and slammed his mouth against hers, his lips bruising and his erection pressed against her belly.

"Xavier," she whispered, though she wasn't sure what she was trying to say.

This wasn't what she was expecting when she came outside to talk to him, but her body seemed to agree with him. She *needed* him to be inside her.

Xavier lifted her into his arms and pressed her against the side of the building, protecting the back of her head with his hand as he did. Sometimes his actions contra-dicted his harsh and demanding personality, but she was beginning to realize that it was all a part of who he was. With her heart beating an unsteady rhythm against her chest, she wrapped her legs around his waist as he pulled her panties off to the side and lined his cock up with her entrance.

"Don't worry, baby," he murmured, smiling against her mouth. "I've got you. But this is going to be fast and hard. You okay with that?"

Her lips parted as she nodded. She hadn't expected it to be anything other than fast and hard for a couple of reasons. One was they were in public, and the other was that they both seemed to need this.

Xavier slammed into her in one swift move, once again stretching her far beyond her limits. She cried out at the sudden invasion, but his mouth muffled the sound so she wouldn't be heard. It hurt, but only for a second, and the pain helped to remind her that this was real, that he wanted her. She was wanted, which was everything to her.

A shudder ran through his body before he braced a hand on the wall and began pounding into her at a punishing pace. The rough brick tore at the skin of her back, his hips slamming into her hard enough that she knew would bruise, but she was too lost in the moment to care about either of those things. She could hear the sounds of everyone else still back in the bar. The music, the laughing, the clattering of glass, everything was continuing like normal while she was getting banged in the alley. And maybe it was the risk of getting caught, but she found it exhilarating and hot as hell.

Madelyn clung to his neck as he moved her on his shaft, the angle pushing him deeper than before. Her walls clenched as he groaned against her mouth, and his hand came down off the wall to circle her neck. She gasped as he applied a little bit of pressure against her throat before he dragged his teeth along her jaw. The sounds of their fucking filled the alley, drowning out everything else.

All of a sudden, the back door to the bar opened, and one of the bartenders stepped outside to throw away a bag of trash. Madelyn gasped and attempted to climb off of Xavier, but he just covered her mouth with his hand as he slowed his movements instead. He continued to fuck her slowly and silently, the sudden change in pace creating a fire in her lower abdomen that slowly grew with each thrust of his hips. She watched with wide eyes as the bartender lifted the lid to the dumpster and tossed the bag inside while scrolling through his phone. He was completely oblivious to what was going on just a few feet away, and within a matter of seconds, he was back inside the bar, none the wiser.

The second the door shut behind him, Xavier began slamming into her again with renewed vigor. His soft grunts sounded in her ear, melting her into a puddle as her breath lodged in her throat. The fire in her abdomen exploded, igniting her entire body as her walls began tightening around him once more. With a few more thrusts of his hips, she found herself teetering on the edge but still unable to go over completely.

"Time for you to cum, little dove," he demanded softly.

Before she realized what was happening, his sharp teeth bit into the curve of her neck, breaking the skin, and his hand came up to cover her mouth as she screamed. That sharp bite of pain was enough to send her flying over the edge in an orgasm that shook her down to her very core.

Xavier's jaw tightened on her neck with a low, deep growl, pushing his teeth deeper into her flesh, as he stilled inside of her. She felt every pulse of his cock as he emptied himself into her. Her body trembled, her limbs going limp, and every ounce of energy she had was sapped. Still,

Xavier continued to hold her as though she weighed nothing at all.

For what felt like an eternity, the two of them remained locked in their embrace, her legs around his waist and his face buried in the side of her neck. Reality came flooding back to her all at once, and her cheeks heated as she realized what she had done. She had once again slept with her stalker, in public no less, and had even told him that she'd be willing to give them a try when, just a couple of days ago, she told him to leave her alone. Something had changed between them now, and she wasn't sure she liked it.

"Don't do that," Xavier said, finally releasing her neck and lifting his head to meet her gaze. She realized that he must have sensed some kind of change in her demeanor because she could see the worry in his eyes. "Don't start doubting this already."

With a gentle push to his chest, Madelyn climbed off of him and back onto her own feet, though she was surprised he let her. She winced as he slid out of her and braced a hand on the wall until her legs were steady enough to hold her up on their own.

Instead of responding right away, she busied herself with readjusting her clothing. She hated the fact that she didn't have anything to clean herself up with and was now going to have to go back inside with a pussy full of cum, but it wasn't like she had many options.

"Madelyn," Xavier pressed as he tucked himself back into his jeans.

"I meant what I said," she replied at last, once her mind was clear enough to form actual thoughts. "I… I am willing to give this a try. But, Xavier, I don't believe in soulmates. And I think that, once you realize how broken and messed up I am, you are going to change your mind about me."

"And when I don't?"

Madelyn just sighed and shook her head. He sounded so sure of this, of them. Meanwhile, she had never been sure of anything. Her life was a rollercoaster that she was still trying to navigate. She didn't know how she was supposed to do this.

"Look, I get it," he began, brushing her hair out of her face. "You aren't a shifter, so you don't feel the bond the same way I do. You probably feel some attraction and the desire to be around me, but nothing much stronger than that. For me? It's entirely different. It's… it's an obsession, an addiction. My wolf is devoted to you and you alone. There will never be anyone else for me. Nor do I want anyone else."

That was probably the most she had ever heard him say all at once, and it was a lot to take in and unpack. She pressed her lips together and looked up at him. "One of these days, you are going to have to tell me more about this whole shifter thing."

"What do you wanna know?" he asked, the corner of his lips tilting up slightly.

Madelyn leaned against the wall and folded her arms across her chest before letting out a breath. She had so many questions that she didn't even know where to begin. She knew Melanie and the others were waiting for her to return, but she couldn't pass up the opportunity to finally get some answers. All of this had been driving her crazy for weeks.

Deciding that her friends could wait a little while longer, she figured she'd start with an easy question. "Were you born a shifter?"

With a nod, he settled against the wall next to her

before he stuck his hands into his pockets and propped his foot up on the wall behind him. "Yes."

"How many of you are there?"

"I have no idea," he admitted with a shrug of his shoulders.

"But there are others; it's not just you, right?"

"Right. Rogue shifters are lone wolves though, meaning we don't run with packs or with any other shifter. I became a rogue after I killed my father, but I had been born into a pack. There were sixty-five of us in that pack, though there are dozens more all over the world."

Madelyn nodded, taking in that information. That was a lot of shifters, and the fact that no one knew they even existed was mind-boggling. "How have you guys remained hidden for so long?"

"Easy," he said. "We learn to control our wolves at a very early age. We stick to small towns that are surrounded by woods so that, when we do let our wolves out, it's not so conspicuous, and it's easier to hide. We stay away from cities where it's harder for us to let our wolves out, and if someone did stumble across one of us, while we were in the middle of shifting or something, we'd just take care of them."

"Meaning you killed them," she clarified.

He nodded again. "They'd be considered a threat, so yeah. We killed them. We'd make it fast though so they didn't suffer, and then we'd either make it look like an accident or make the body disappear entirely. Packs never killed lightly though. They'd try talking to the person first, explaining the situation, and assessing the risks."

"Do, uh, do I need to be worried?" she asked hesitantly, not sure she wanted to know the answer. By all accounts, she would be considered a threat now since she knew about the existence of shifters.

Thankfully, Xavier shook his head and she was able to relax a bit. "No, little dove. You do not need to be worried. You are my mate. You were going to find out eventually. Many shifters take human mates. They just have to make sure that their mate is in a position to accept them and their secret before they tell them."

"But you didn't do that with me," she muttered. "You didn't wait."

"I tried, but I wasn't given a choice, no," he explained. "Colby threatened you. And then that junkie tried to kill you. Your safety is my number one priority because, if anything happens to you, I die. That's how strong the bond is for me. So, I took the risk, even knowing there was a possibility that you could expose the existence of my kind."

When she found out what he was, she had been angry that he had kept it from her, especially since they had slept together. But after taking the time to really think about it, she realized it made sense. It was a big secret, one that couldn't be trusted to just anyone.

So, her being angry with him for not trusting her had been completely unwarranted because he *had* trusted her. He had shown his true self to her before he knew if she was ready to hear it, which made her feel like a jerk for ignoring him for the last two days.

"Tell me more about the fated mate thing," she said after a while.

If he was getting annoyed with her questions, he didn't let on. "To be honest, I thought it was a myth. It's been a long time since I've heard of a shifter finding their fated mate, but since I don't really associate with any others of my kind, it makes sense that I hadn't heard anything. When a shifter sees his fated mate for the first time, he knows it immediately. It's this strong, undeniable pull that leads you to this person, and a bond forms between you and them, one that's said to strengthen over time. It's like a flashing neon sign that screams that this is the person you are supposed to spend the rest of your life with. The one person who's your absolute perfect fit."

"Soulmates," she whispered.

Xavier looked at her and nodded. "Yes. And that person? Our soulmate? They become everything to us. They become our life, our will to live, and we would do anything and everything to protect them. They are all that matter in the world. And because shifters are mainly social creatures, we can't be away from them for too long, or we start to lose our minds. We go feral and have to be put down, or we become a menace. And if they reject us? It's an instant death sentence."

"Which is why you started stalking me," she sighed, thumping her head back against the wall. The more she learned, the more everything seemed to fall into place. The more it all made sense.

Xavier wasn't trying to be creepy or weird. He just couldn't stay away from her without losing his marbles. Granted, he could have approached her like a normal person and struck up a conversation, but considering the way he was brought up, he probably didn't have much by way of social skills.

Looking over at him, Madelyn gently took Xavier's hand in hers. "Thank you for being honest with me. I appreciate it."

"I've never lied to you, little dove," he stated, giving her hand a gentle squeeze. "I may have kept things from you, but that was only because I needed to be sure. Now that you know the truth, I won't keep things from you anymore."

"Good, because I'm going to have more questions for you."

He chuckled softly. "I'd expect nothing less."

"And you need to stop stalking me too," she added as the thought crossed her mind. "If you want this to work, you need to start acting like a normal person. Take me out on dates and stuff."

A panty-dropping smirk splayed across his lips as he yanked on her hand, pulling her toward him. "Do you want to start tonight? Do you want to take me inside and introduce me to your friends then?"

Madelyn laughed and shook her head. "Uh, no. Not tonight. I need to figure out how to tell Melanie about all this first."

"So, you are just going to go back in there after disappearing for a half hour, all by yourself, and with a fresh shifter mark on your neck and a pussy full of baby batter?"

His words made her wince and her nose crinkled in disgust. She had heard it called many things, but that was by far the worst of them all. "Ew, don't ever call it that. That's just gross."

His chest rumbled with his laughter as Xavier pressed a kiss to the top of her head. "Alright, sorry."

"Wait," she said after a moment, "What do you mean 'shifter's mark'?"

His smile grew as he reached up and brushed his fingers along the bite mark on her neck. "This is a shifter's mark. Because each bite mark is unique to the shifter that gave it, shifters bite their mates as a way to claim them as their own."

"So, you marked me."

"Yes."

Pressing her lips together, her eyes narrowed at him. "I oughta slap you."

"You tried that once already. Remember how it turned out?" he teased playfully.

Chapter Thirteen

Xavier

A few minutes later, Xavier was pulling out of the parking lot of the bar and heading back toward his place. He had wanted to stay to spend more time with Madelyn, but she told him that she wasn't ready to introduce him to her friends yet. So, he decided against forcing the issue. There was plenty of time for that now that she had finally agreed to be his and due to the fact that she now bore his mark.

A smile crossed his face as he drove down the highway, turning his thoughts to all the questions she had thrown at him instead of how horrible it felt to be away from her. He hadn't minded them that all because he knew that was her way of trying to get to know him better and coming to grips with the fact that she had agreed to be his. It was a promising sign and gave him hope that she wanted to make this work as much as he did. Not that she had much of a choice anymore. A shifter's mark was irreversible.

Normally, a shifter would get permission from their mate before he marked her, but he didn't regret it in the slightest. The bond between them was solid now, meaning that she was his—mind, body, and soul—and it was that knowledge that kept a smile firmly planted on his face as he drove the rest of the way home.

The house he owned was about two miles outside of Cedarwood. He liked his privacy and still wanted to keep some distance between himself and the townsfolk, just in case. It was a little further away from Madelyn than he would have liked, but he had bought it before he met her.

It wasn't much, just three bedrooms and two bathrooms, but it was what he had needed at the time. He had one of the spare rooms set up as a small home gym, and the other was an office of sorts. The house sat on a couple of acres and was surrounded by forests, so he had plenty of space to run and let his wolf free, which was exactly what he planned on doing when he got home to blow off some steam and keep himself occupied until he could see his mate again.

His cell phone rang in the center console, and he reached for it, wondering if his stubborn and beautiful mate was missing him already. However, the number on the caller ID was listed as unavailable, and his smile fell as he answered the call.

"Yeah."

"Xavier," the familiar gruff voice stated on the other end of the line. "It's Rodrigo."

Even without the introduction, Xavier knew who it was. He grew up hearing that voice every single day, and even though he was out now, it still seemed to have the same effect on him. His entire body went rigid, the muscles in his back stiffening, his spine straightening, and the knuckles on his left hand tightening on the steering wheel.

"Yes, sir."

"Come now, Xavier. You are no longer under my command. There's no need to be so formal."

Xavier's jaw ticked at Rodrigo's playful tone. It felt like a trap, as did the phone call. Rodrigo always commanded respect, even from him and Isabelle. So, he decided to ignore his request. "What can I do for you, sir?"

Rodrigo sighed through the phone. "We have a bit of a problem. With Colby."

"Yeah, I'm aware. Isabelle stopped by and told me that he put a mark on me."

"Oh, I'm not worried about that," Rodrigo told him quickly. "I know you can handle him. I'm talking about the fact that he somehow found out about you and what you are."

That was one thing that he didn't miss about his time with the Cortez Family. Rumors and things always spread like wildfire. He was willing to bet that *everyone* in the family knew what he was now, which could potentially be problematic.

Cursing himself and his lack of forethought, he turned onto the gravel drive that led to his place. "He found out because I shifted in front of him."

"And why would you do that?" Rodrigo asked, a hint of irritation in his voice. "You always said that no one was supposed to know."

"And they're not," he replied shortly. "I just didn't have a choice."

"I don't understand."

Xavier put the car in Park and killed the engine before heading inside. After closing the door behind him, he dropped his keys and his wallet into the small bowl on the entry table. He was now facing the same dilemma he had faced when Isabelle had shown up at the bistro.

Both he and Isabelle were ruthless and damn good killers. They could torture a person to the brink of death and yet keep them alive for days. They were talented, skilled, experts in their field, and yet, Rodrigo was so much worse than either one of them. He hadn't wanted *anyone* from his old life to know about Madelyn, and it was bad enough that Colby had found out. The thought of informing Rodrigo as well rattled him.

Because of this, Xavier headed into the office and flipped on the light. All at once, fourteen monitors flicked to life on the far wall. He made his way over to the desk and hit a few keys, bringing up the security cameras for Iggy's bar. Like the police station, the security protocols at Iggy's were way too easy for him to get around. He found Madelyn immediately.

She was still sitting at the same table with her friends. She was laughing and having a good time, which made him smile as he brushed his fingers against the screen. She had pulled her sweater up to hide his mark, but he understood the reason behind that. He just wished he could see it on her again as he didn't have enough time to admire it before she went back inside.

"Xavier."

He shook his head, focusing once again on the call. "What?"

"Are you going to tell me why you lost control and revealed yourself to Colby?"

There was no getting around this, he knew that. Rodrigo was going to keep pushing him until he got his answers, and he always did know what buttons to push to get them. In order to avoid all that, he was going to have to tell him. It would be better if Rodrigo found out from him instead of someone else.

"Colby threatened someone important to me," he stated simply. "And you know I don't take too kindly to people threatening what's mine."

There was a thick pause on the other end of the phone while Rodrigo processed what he had told him. While he waited, Xavier watched as Madelyn and her friends got up from the table, clearly ready to leave the bar. He hit a few more keys on the keyboard and brought up a cell phone tracking app before typing in her number. Since Melanie had picked her up, he couldn't track her car.

"She must be important if you revealed your deepest secret to Colby to protect her," Rodrigo stated after a while.

"Yes, sir," he replied. "If you don't mind my asking, how did you find out about Colby discovering what I am?"

"Well, therein lies the problem. Colby started running his mouth to the rest of the family," Rodrigo explained, further confirming his suspicions. "Most didn't care because they knew you and were just grateful that you were on our side. However, there are a few who are angry. They feel betrayed that I allowed someone like you among our ranks. Those who feel that way have disappeared, no doubt making their way to meet up with Colby so they can help him take you out."

Xavier ground his teeth together in irritation, pinching the bridge of his nose. He wasn't worried about Colby; the guy was an ass but nowhere near Xavier's level. He could handle him easily. He could probably handle the others as well. It just made things way more complicated than they needed to be. And if Colby told them about Madelyn, which was highly likely, then she, too, would be in danger, and he couldn't have that.

"I've sent some of the guys and Isabelle to help. They

have orders to kill the traitors on sight, and I wanted to give you a heads up," Rodrigo continued when Xavier didn't respond.

"No!" he snapped, sitting up straighter. "I can handle this myself, Rodrigo."

The thought of so many trained killers so close to Madelyn sent him into a panic. It was a feeling he wasn't used to but one he was not going to ignore. There was bound to be some collateral damage, and he would be damned if he was going to let that be his mate.

"No offense, Xavier," Rodrigo said calmly, "but this isn't your call. These guys disobeyed a direct order. They disrespected me. This is my problem now, and I intend to clean it up."

"Then you should know, sir, I will destroy anyone who puts my mate in danger. Whether they are part of the family or not."

Rodrigo clicked his tongue. "You know we do not harm innocents."

Xavier chuckled darkly. "No, but there is always collateral damage. And Colby was willing to shoot her so that she wasn't a witness to his killing me. There are flaws in the rules, Rodrigo. Flaws that guys like Colby can exploit to get away with whatever they want. I won't let her get caught in the middle of your war."

He could practically hear Rodrigo grinding his teeth through the phone. He had never spoken so brashly to the guy before; he had only ever been respectful. Rodrigo hated not having control because he felt it lessened his power, but he needed to know that he was not as in control as he believed he was.

"They will only be after the traitors and Colby, who I've deemed a traitor as well. You can help if you wish, but make sure you keep your *mate* out of the way. Just to be safe."

"That sounds an awful lot like a threat," he pointed out, watching the little dot on the screen that was Madelyn pulling into her house. He quickly switched to the camera feeds inside her place to make sure it was clear for her.

"It's not a threat, Xavier," Rodrigo spat. "It's just fact. I need to keep my family in line, a family that you no longer wanted to be a part of. If you don't want anything to happen to your precious mate, then you'd do well to stay out of our way. Is that going to be a problem?"

"Not at all," he replied. "But as I said, *anyone* who threatens her is a dead man. So, you better make sure they follow their orders to the letter."

The phone went silent for quite some time. Xavier had even pulled it away from his ear to make sure that the call was still connected. However, after a while, he heard Rodrigo sigh again. "How did we get here, Xavier? How has our relationship come to this?"

Xavier leaned back in his chair, his eyes locked on Madelyn as she moved into her bathroom, no doubt to take a shower to clean up the mess he had left behind during their time in the alley.

"I don't know," he replied carefully. "I hold no ill will toward you, Rodrigo, and I will always be grateful to you and for everything you did for me."

"But you found yourself a new family, it seems," Rodrigo added softly, "in this Madelyn."

"I have," he agreed with a small nod of his head.

"And she is important to you?"

"The most important thing to me," he corrected matter-of-factly. "I would die for her."

He was admitting far more than he'd like to admit to a

skilled killer, but there was no point in keeping it from him. Now that Rodrigo knew about Madelyn, he had the right to know how far Xavier would go to keep her safe.

"Well, I'm happy for you, son. Truly."

"You are?" he asked. He didn't mean to sound so surprised. He just wasn't used to hearing stuff like that from someone like him.

Rodrigo believed that emotions were a sign of weakness, and in all the years Xavier had known him, he had never heard him say anything like that. To anyone. He didn't even think Rodrigo had ever told Isabelle that he loved her, and she was his only child.

"Of course I am," Rodrigo replied with a chuckle. "I've always known that you deserved better than this life of violence and bloodshed. Isabelle was born into it; you were not."

"But you… you raised me to be who I am. You trained me to be—"

"I only did what you asked me to do, Xavier," Rodrigo interrupted. "You asked me to give your life a purpose, a meaning, and you always wanted to do whatever Isabelle was doing. Since I saw a lot of myself in you, I couldn't say no to you. But I've always wanted you to have better. Why do you think I let you leave? No one leaves. You know that."

Xavier pressed his lips together. "I did wonder about that."

"Well, now you know. Look, I can't ask the guys to protect your girl, but I can tell them to be on the lookout and to make sure that she's not injured or killed by any one of us."

"Make sure that you do," Xavier replied. "I'd hate for us to have to end on such bad terms."

It wasn't perfect, and there was still the chance that

something could happen to Madelyn if he wasn't careful and didn't keep her out of danger, but he would do whatever it took to make sure that didn't happen.

He guessed the police were going to have a lot more cases on their hands because it appeared as though war was coming to Cedarwood.

Chapter Fourteen

Madelyn

The next evening, Madelyn was sitting on the couch in her living room with her feet tucked up beneath her while having a glass of wine with Melanie. She had asked Melanie to come by because she felt that it was finally time for her to tell her friend about Xavier.

This was not going to be an easy conversation to have, and Madelyn had made herself sick thinking about it all day. It was going to be hard to get her to understand when she couldn't tell her that Xavier was a shifter or that he believed that the two of them were fated to be together. However, she had kept things from Melanie for long enough. Besides, if she and Xavier were going to attempt to be a normal couple, even though the two of them were anything but, she needed to be able to go out with him in public. So, she owed it to Melanie to give her a heads-up.

"Okay, I say this with all the love in my heart," Melanie commented, setting her wine down on the coffee table.

"But you look like you are either about to throw up or pass out. What's going on? Is everything okay?"

Madelyn gave her friend a weak attempt at a smile. "Yeah, I'm okay. I just…" She swallowed hard as she leaned over and set her own glass down. "There's something that I need to talk to you about, and it's probably going to be hard for you to understand."

"Okay," Melanic drawled out the word. "Because that's not ominous or anything."

"I know," she agreed with a small nod. "I just don't know how to say it. It's not going to be an easy conversation."

"Now you are just freaking me out. Spit it out already."

Madelyn chewed on the inside of her cheek briefly. "Alright. Well, I… I met someone. A guy, I mean. He's… he's hot as hell, over-protective, likes to take control, and is all sorts of wrong for me. But the connection between us is really freaking strong and difficult to ignore. So, we, uh, we decided to see where it goes."

Melanie studied her for a moment, a look of pure confusion on her face. "Alright. While I'm not fond of the idea of you dating someone that you claim is 'all sorts of wrong for you', I am glad that you are getting back out there again. I was worried there for a bit after David. But, I still don't see what the big deal is. Why did you assume that would be difficult for me to understand?"

"His name is Xavier, Mel," Madelyn added quickly, knowing she needed to get it out before she chickened out.

It was almost comical how Madelyn could pinpoint the exact moment that the dots connected together in Melanie's brain. Her eyes widened, and her face turned a shade of pink that Madelyn had never seen before. Whether it was surprise or anger, she didn't know.

"Xavier," Melanie said slowly. "As in…"

"As in my… my stalker," she finished for her.

Melanie was on her feet so fast that Madelyn flinched in response. That was nothing compared to the anger in Melanie's voice as she completely went off on her.

"Are you out of your fucking mind?" she exclaimed loudly. "What the hell are you thinking? Or are you even thinking at all?"

"Melanie, I—"

"No, just stop. I don't want to hear how you are fucking rationalizing this shit in your head. He's your fucking stalker, Madelyn. He put David in the hospital just for talking to you! He's a monster. Who knows what else that guy has done?" Melanie paced in front of the coffee table, the vein in her temple throbbing. Madelyn had known that she wasn't going to take the news very well, but she didn't expect her to blow up like this. "I mean, the guy should be in prison! And there was a time when you agreed with me on that!"

"That was before I knew him, Mel," she tried to explain, though her voice was soft. "He's really not that bad of a guy, and I—"

"Oh, you think you know him now? You think you know everything there is to know about him? About his past, his likes, his dislikes, how many people he's killed?"

Madelyn sighed heavily. "No, I don't know *everything* about him, but I know enough. Look, he may have gone about this the wrong way, but I wasn't lying about the connection that—"

"Oh, for God's sake, Madelyn, there is no fucking connection!" Melanie screamed at her. "There can't be. And you are delusional if you think there is."

Melanie's words felt like a punch to the gut. She never expected to hear something like that from someone she considered to be her best friend. Especially someone she had confided in about her past.

This time though, Madelyn knew she wasn't delusional. She knew what she felt, and she was fairly confident in her decision to let it play out. She was a bit ashamed to admit it, but she wanted to see if there was anything to the whole fated mate thing. It sounded way too good to be true, but she had thought shifters were fictional too. Her being his fated mate would explain why she was so drawn to a guy like him.

"Are you going to let me explain things, or are you just going to keep freaking out on me?" she asked pointedly.

Melanie spun on her. "Explain what, exactly? This guy is going to end up killing you, you know, and then I am going to be the one who has to solve your murder. But hey, at least, it will be an easy close."

"Come on, Melanie," Madelyn tried again.

Melanie laughed and shook her head. "Nope. I'm not doing it."

Madelyn jumped to her feet as Melanie slid on her shoes and stormed toward the door. She snatched her jacket off the hook and yanked it on.

"Mel, wait. Please," Madelyn pleaded.

"No, Madelyn. I'm done. I can't do this." She turned to Madelyn as she entered the foyer. "I am not going to stand by and watch you get yourself killed. I can't. And I suggest you go and get your head checked out because there is something seriously fucking wrong with you."

Madelyn's heart plummeted into the pit of her stomach as she watched Melanie leave. Her best friend, who had sworn that nothing she told her would change things between them only days before, had essentially just ended their friendship. She had done so without letting Madelyn try to explain how she felt or why she had made the decision to give Xavier a chance. It had been all too easy for Melanie to turn her back on her. While she had expected some resistance, expected her to be angry and upset, and maybe even try to talk her out of it, she never once thought that Melanie would do this.

Madelyn closed her eyes, a few tears rolling down her cheeks as she turned and reluctantly set the alarm.

"You didn't tell her the truth," the now familiar voice stated from behind her. "About what I am or what you are to me."

Madelyn turned to see Xavier leaning against the door frame leading into the kitchen, a full duffel bag on his shoulder. She wasn't surprised he was there as he seemed to like to randomly appear wherever she was. In fact, she was kind of grateful for that now as it made her feel less alone.

"No, I didn't," she replied, going back into the living room to grab the glasses and the wine bottle to take them back into the kitchen.

Xavier followed, dropping his bag by the chair. "Why?"

"It's not my secret to tell," she said honestly, tears still stinging the backs of her eyes. "Besides, you said no one is supposed to know. I didn't want to break some kind of sacred shifter rule."

Massive arms wrapped around her waist as he pressed a kiss to the curve of her neck, right over the bite mark he had left on her. "Yeah, well, I seem to be breaking all kinds of rules for you, little dove. What's one more to add to the list?"

Madelyn's fingers gripped the edge of the sink as she shook her head. "She wouldn't have believed me anyway, Xavier. I wouldn't have either if I were in her shoes. The only reason I do believe it is because I saw it with my own eyes."

"I can always show her if you like."

She turned in his arms so that she could look into his beautiful eyes. "I appreciate that, but I don't think you could get anywhere near her without her arresting you." She rested her forehead against his chest, a few more tears escaping. "I knew she was going to be upset about this, but I didn't think she would actually cut me off. I thought we were closer than that."

"I'm sorry," he told her.

She scoffed a laugh. "No, you're not. You knew she was a cop; you had to know something like this would happen. You have to know how cops feel about stalking, and yet you pursued me that way anyway."

Xavier lifted her chin with his fingers. "You misunderstand me, Madelyn. You're right to assume that I'm not sorry I pursued you or that I marked you as mine. I'm not even sorry about Melanie as she clearly wasn't as good a friend as you believed her to be. However, I am sorry that you are going through this and that you lost someone you care about. I know how much she meant to you."

Madelyn pressed her lips together, a fresh wave of emotion washing over her. "I knew the risks when I agreed to this."

This was getting to be too much, and she needed to change the subject. Otherwise, she would completely fall apart and would end up spending the rest of the night bawling her eyes out. She didn't have the mental capacity for all that at the moment. She also didn't want to pass up the opportunity to find out more about the mystery that was Xavier. Melanie was right about one thing: She didn't know nearly enough about him.

Stepping out of his arms, Madelyn moved back toward the living room where the two of them took a seat on the couch. "What's with the bag?" she asked him curiously. "You going somewhere?"

Jaw clenching, Xavier shook his head. "No. I'm going to be staying here with you for a while."

She sighed and pinched the bridge of her nose. "Okay, I know I agreed to give this a shot, but that doesn't mean you can just move in here, Xavier."

He turned his body on the couch to face her, cocking an eyebrow. "First of all, I told you, if we do this, we are doing this. You already bear my mark; there's no taking it back. It's permanent, and so is this. Secondly, that's not why I'm staying here."

"Then why are you?" While she had plenty of things to say about him automatically assuming that they were permanent, as well as his marking her the way he had without permission, she felt that figuring out why he was insisting on staying with her was more important.

"Remember Colby?"

She nodded. "As if I could forget. You think he's going to come after me?"

"There's a good chance, and it won't be just him either. Not anymore."

"What do you mean?"

Xavier ran his fingers through his hair. "After I revealed the fact that I was a shifter to him, he went back and told the rest of the family."

"The Cortez family?" she asked.

He nodded curtly. "The only people who knew what I was were Rodrigo and Isabelle. I guess a lot of the guys got pissed when Colby told them. They rebelled against Rodrigo and left to hunt me alongside Colby. Rodrigo is pissed and labeled them as traitors. So now, war is on its way to Cedarwood."

Madelyn didn't like the sound of that at all. There was

a good chance that a lot of innocent people could end up getting hurt just because they were in the wrong place at the wrong time. Collateral damage.

"But what does that have to do with me?"

Reaching forward, Xavier cupped the side of her neck. "Because you are my mate, hurting you would weaken me. It would make it easier for them to kill me. The bond between us affects me more than it does you. If anything happens to you, it will destroy me."

Madelyn couldn't help but wonder if that was true. If she was so important to Xavier that, if anything happened to her, it would physically affect him. She had never been important to someone before, and the thought caused her heart to squeeze in her chest.

"But if they didn't know about shifters, how would they know that?"

"They wouldn't, not for sure," he responded. "But I already revealed my hand to Colby that day he threatened you. It wouldn't be hard for him to figure out, and I'm not taking any chances. Not with you."

Madelyn pulled her bottom lip in between her teeth as she wrung her hands in her lap. It looked as though she was going to have a new roommate.

Chapter Fifteen

Xavier

Xavier was lying against the headboard on Madelyn's bed while she changed, washed her face, and brushed her teeth. He had already changed into a pair of sweats himself, which was new for him as he usually slept naked. Since she was allowing him to stay in her bed, not that he gave her much of a choice in the matter, he wasn't going to push it too far just yet.

He could honestly say that he was surprised that she hadn't put up more of a fight when he told her he would be staying with her. It wouldn't have made a difference since her life was on the line, but he hadn't expected her to give in so easily. He guessed she understood how dire the situation was, which was good. She had only recently stopped fighting him so much, and he didn't want to go back to that.

"So, how long were you with Isabelle?" Madelyn called from the bathroom.

He chuckled and shook his head. She was trying to make it seem like a casual question, but he could hear the bite of jealousy in her voice.

Over the last couple of hours, he had answered every question she had about shifters and his time with the Cortez family, refusing to lie or keep things from her any longer. It wasn't what he was used to doing, opening up like that, but for her, he vowed to make the effort. It hadn't been easy, and he had ended up telling her a lot more than he thought he was capable of.

It felt as though she had sliced him open to expose his very soul. He told her about his kills, about the torture he inflicted, and he told her a bit more about the monster hiding inside of him with the insatiable bloodlust. He had thought that knowledge would make her run for the hills, and he wouldn't have blamed her for it, but instead, she seemed to accept it as a part of him.

It did not go unnoticed though that she tended to get a bit squirrelly whenever he brought up Isabelle, and he had wondered when she was going to ask about her directly.

"We were never together," he replied. "Not in a relationship anyway."

The bathroom door opened, and Madelyn stepped out looking good enough to eat. She had pulled her hair up into a messy bun, her face was freshly washed, and she was wearing short sleep shorts and a tank top with no bra underneath. Even in the dim light, he could see her nipples peeking through the thin material of her shirt, and his mouth watered.

"But you slept with her," she stated pointedly.

He shrugged as his eyes drank her in, his sweats doing nothing to hide how much he liked what he saw. "Yeah, but it was just a way for us to blow off steam, to scratch an itch. There were never any emotions behind it. Two people don't have to be together to fuck."

"Maybe there were no emotions for you," she said as she climbed into the bed and sat in the middle of the mattress, next to his hip, while tucking her feet beneath her. "But Colby said that it broke her heart when you left."

Xavier snorted. "Colby is a fucking liar."

"Maybe. But you also said that Colby may want to hurt me in order to hurt you. He knew you were into me before he found out you were a shifter. What if he told me about her to make me doubt this? Doubt us?"

"I'm sure he did," he agreed easily. He wouldn't put it past Colby to do just that. "But that doesn't mean he was telling the truth. There was never anything other than sex between Isabelle and me, so you have nothing to worry about."

"I'm not worried," she said quickly, the tone of her voice giving her away.

He chuckled, not believing her for a second. "Whatever you say, Madelyn."

She rolled her eyes but couldn't hide the blush that crept to her cheeks. "Okay, I think it's time we talk about you marking me the way you did."

Unable to go another minute without touching her in some way, Xavier lunged forward and pushed her down onto the bed, his hips settling between her legs. "No. No more talking."

"Xavier," she said seriously.

He sighed. It wasn't that he was trying to avoid the conversation. He just didn't see the point of it. He already told her why he did it, and there was no taking it back. Besides, there were other things that he wanted to do much more than talk, like burying himself in her tight little pussy.

"It's already done, so there's not much to talk about, is there, little dove?"

"Yes, there is. I only said that I would give this a shot. But you went and marked me, something you claim is permanent. Why?"

"Because you are mine," he said simply. "And you will always be mine."

Her eyebrows shot up. "So, I don't get a choice in the matter?"

"You would have chosen me anyway. I just skipped past all the bullshit."

"You don't know that for sure." Despite her words, she wrapped her arms around his neck while worrying her lip in between her teeth. "I could still change my mind about us."

A grin spread across his lips as he shook his head and nipped at her jaw. "No. You couldn't."

He watched as her lips pressed into a thin line, her eyes bouncing between his. He was silently daring her to deny what they both already knew to be true. She couldn't change her mind about him any more than he could change his about her. The fact that she was still trying to do so was irritating.

Thankfully, she seemed to think better of fighting him on it. She sighed heavily. "Well, no, I couldn't. Not now—you made sure of that," she relented softly as he began trailing kisses down the side of her neck. He loved the moan that came out of her because of it. She was always so receptive to him, and it drove him crazy, knowing that he held all the power. "Are we crazy? I mean, this is... this is so unconventional."

Lifting his head, he met her eyes. "Yes, we are absolutely crazy. But who the fuck cares? This here"—he motioned between the two of them with his hand—"it's between us. No one else. Now, are you done with all the questions? I'd like to get back to what I was doing."

With an adorable giggle, Madelyn nodded, and he crushed his lips against hers. His dick hardened as his hand slid down her body, and he gripped her breasts, her hips, her ass, anything he could get his hands on. It didn't matter how many times he touched her, it would never be enough. She was the only one who could tame the beast inside of him and bring him to heal. As startling as it was, he realized that *she* might actually be the one with all the power because, until now, no one had been able to silence the bloodlust that ran rampant within his mind.

A whisper of a moan escaped her lips as her fingers tugged on his hair, her back bowing against him. The restraint he had on the monster within him snapped, and he growled low before pushing himself off of her.

Madelyn dropped back to the bed, her chest heaving as she tracked him with her eyes while he climbed off the bed and crossed the room to his bag, which was sitting on the bay window.

"Xavier, what are you—"

"Patience, little dove," he crooned. "I have a little surprise for you."

He dug inside his duffel bag, letting several things spill over the sides of it and onto the bench seat, until he found what he was looking for. A mischievous grin played across his mouth before he returned to the edge of the bed, setting the items on the mattress and stripping out of his sweats.

"Take your clothes off and move up toward the head-board," he demanded, his voice low.

She blinked at him for a moment before scrambling to do as she was told. She yanked her shirt up over her head and shimmied out of her shorts before tossing them both onto the ground and then moving up toward the headboard. He climbed back onto the bed, straddling her thighs with his belt in his hands.

"Give me your wrists."

Once again, she did as she was told and held her wrists out toward him. His lips quirked up at the side as he folded the belt into a figure-eight and slipped it over her hands. He pulled the strap, tightening the make-shift restraint onto her wrists, and then secured it to the headboard. When he was done, he gave it a firm tug to make sure that it would hold.

Sitting back, he admired the view of her all trussed up and ready for the taking. With her arms tied up over her head, her breasts were pushed out, rising and falling with every breath she took and just begging to be sucked on. Her silky hair was fanned out on the pillow, framing her beautiful face. She was the picture of perfection, and she was all his.

He trailed his fingertips down her outstretched arms and watched the goosebumps rise on her flesh. "Fuck, Madelyn, you are so damn beautiful, baby."

"Xavier," she gasped, squirming beneath his touch.

"Patience," he soothed, his fingers continuing their exploration. "This is the first time you've let me in your room willingly. And I plan on taking full advantage of that."

Reaching over, Xavier picked up the second item he had pulled out of his bag, a small black box. He winked at her as he opened it and pulled out what was tucked inside before discarding the box on the ground. The metal was cool against his overheated skin, and the deep purple gem glinted in the soft light of the room. He held it up so that she could see it.

"Do you know what this is?" he asked, thoroughly

enjoying the way her eyes widened at the sight of the butt plug in his hand.

She licked her lips and nodded hesitantly. "Yes, but—"

He rubbed her thigh with his free hand reassuringly. "Relax. It's just a small one."

As he spoke, he began running the plug down her chest, between her breasts, and over her stomach slowly. He could tell that she was holding her breath as if nervous or scared. Knowing that he needed to get her to relax, he brought it down further and began circling her clit with it. She gasped, her arms tugging on the restraints, as he shifted to settle himself between her thighs, holding them apart.

"I want to take your ass, little dove," he told her simply. "I want to claim every part of you. Have you ever done that before?"

She shook her head, nearly making him groan knowing that he'd be the first one to claim her ass.

"Yeah, I didn't think so. Which is why I brought this," he told her. "If you are going to take my cock, we need to work our way up to it. But again, we are starting small."

Gently, he pushed the plug into her pussy, soaking it with her arousal. Her breath caught in her throat as she attempted to close her legs, but his position wouldn't allow her to do so. He continued to pump it in and out of her a few times, taking his time and allowing her to get used to the feel of it inside of her. When it was fully lubricated, he pulled it out of her and moved it further down to her puckered hole. Her whole body stiffened, and her eyes flew open.

"Xavier, w-wait," she stammered.

"Easy, little dove," he soothed, gently pressing on her lower abdomen to keep her still. "Do you trust me?"

Her tongue darted out to wet her lips before she gave him a quick nod.

"Then believe me when I tell you that you can take it. I'll take it slow. I just need you to relax for me. Think you can do that?"

She gave him another small nod. "Yes."

"Yes, what?"

"Yes, sir," she breathed as her muscles began to ease beneath him.

The corner of his lips tilted up, and he applied a little pressure to the plug. The end pushed through the tight ring of muscles, causing her body to tense again.

He leaned forward and brushed his lips against hers. "Relax, Madelyn. Breathe. I've got you."

Giving her a moment to adjust and get used to the intrusion was pure torture for him. He wasn't usually a gentle man, he didn't take things slow, but the thought of hurting her made him sick to his stomach. He wanted her to enjoy this just as much as he was.

When she was as relaxed as she was going to get, he pushed the plug the rest of the way in with a groan. "Good girl," he praised.

Madelyn's back flew off the mattress, her lips pressed into a thin line. The leather of the belt strained against the metal posts in the headboard. He dropped his head, kissing up her thigh and along the length of her body. When he reached her lips, his tongue dove into her mouth as his hand came up and collared her throat. She continued to squirm beneath him, no doubt trying to get used to the plug in her ass, and he tweaked her nipple to add to the sensation as he lined himself up with her pussy.

When she moaned into his mouth, he couldn't wait any longer. He thrust into her in a single move and growled loudly at the feel of it. Even though it was a smaller plug, he could still feel it pressing against his cock. They were definitely going to have to work her up to be able to take him.

"Fuck, Xavier," she moaned. "So full."

"You can take it, little dove," he ground out through clenched teeth.

He began picking up the pace, slamming into her harder and harder as he lost himself completely. His grip on her throat tightened as he kissed her. Madelyn tried to reach for him, but the restraints held firm, and the sight of her completely at his mercy was like a dream come true. He could do whatever he wanted to her, and there was nothing she could do to stop him.

The bedframe shook with the intensity of his thrusts, and Madelyn's moans grew louder. The fingers on his hand pressed against the pulse of her neck, feeling the rapid beat of her heart patter against his fingertips, matching his own. Her walls began to tighten around him, along with the increased pressure of the plug, and his hips snapped against hers as he chased the high. The sound of skin slapping against skin filled the room as sweat began to bead along his lower back.

Time stopped meaning anything to him as he lost himself in Madelyn's body. His lips moved from her neck to her chest, once again marking her with hickeys and soft little bites. Deciding he wanted a different angle, he pulled out of her completely, making her whimper, before he grabbed her hips and flipped her onto her belly.

Madelyn scrambled onto her knees the best she could without the use of her hands, and he slammed into her again, making her cry out as her hands gripped the bars of the headboard. His palm collided with her ass hard, and her walls gripped him tightly in response. He groaned and smacked it again.

With the deeper angle and the sight of the plug in her ass, he knew he wasn't going to last much longer. He reached around until his fingers found her clit, and he began circling it with heavy strokes.

"Oh, fuck," Madelyn gasped as her walls began to quiver around him.

"That's it, baby. Cum for me."

With a few more thrusts, she screamed his name as she came around him, her pussy clenching tightly. He slammed into her hard and came right alongside her with a roar. He felt every pulse of his cock as he emptied himself inside of her.

Pressing a soft kiss to her sweaty shoulder, Xavier reached forward and quickly released her from the belt. He pulled out of her and gently pulled the plug out before he collapsed onto the bed, gathering her into his arms. He lifted her wrists to inspect them, grateful that the skin was only a little red.

"Are you okay?" he asked her.

She looked up at him, a small, exhausted smile on her swollen lips. "I can't feel my legs, but yeah. I'm pretty great."

He chuckled and kissed the top of her head before laying her against his chest. He had never actually slept next to someone else before, and he had thought it would be difficult for him to let his guard down enough to fall asleep. But holding Madelyn in his arms, listening to her breathing deepen as she drifted off herself, he quickly found himself relaxing, and his eyes began to close of their own accord.

Chapter Sixteen

Xavier

It was the middle of the night, and Xavier was in the middle of a deep and dreamless sleep, which was a rare occurrence for him. However, that peaceful moment was shattered by what sounded like a sharp whistle coming from outside the house. Jolting awake, he blinked and rubbed the sleep from his eyes, his vision quickly adjusting to the darkness of the room, as he listened for the sound again. Because Madelyn hadn't stirred and was still fast asleep against his side, he was beginning to think that he had imagined it. At least, until the whistle sounded again and drew his attention toward the window.

Gritting his teeth in irritation, he carefully pulled his arm out from beneath Madelyn's head, not wanting to wake her. He silently climbed out of bed and padded his way to the window, not caring about his current nakedness, before looking out into the night. Unsurprisingly, Colby was there, standing out on the lawn with a smirk on his freshly scarred face.

Unlike the last time Xavier saw the guy, Colby wasn't pissing himself in fear. Instead, he seemed a bit cocky, which led him to believe that he wasn't here alone. There was a very high probability that the others who had deflected from the 'Family' were hiding among the trees, waiting to ambush him, and the fact that they had come to Madelyn's house to do so really pissed him off too.

"Hey, *freak*," Colby sneered, his voice drifting up to Xavier through the glass. "Didn't think you got rid of me that easily, did you?"

It took Xavier a moment to realize that Colby hadn't bothered to raise his voice, which meant he really *was* losing his touch. It shouldn't have taken him so long to realize such an important detail.

It was clear that Colby had done some research since he discovered what Xavier was. Xavier just wasn't sure how. As far as he knew, there wasn't any literature or websites on the traits of his kind. The only person he knew who had that kind of information was Rodrigo, and he wasn't the type to run his mouth or divulge secrets, even if they weren't on the best of terms. He made a mental note to check out how Colby got his information later since it didn't matter much at the moment.

"It's time we finish this, Xavier," Colby continued when he hadn't reacted. "Come down here and face me, or so help me God, I will burn this place to the ground with you and your little girlfriend inside."

Colby turned and began heading into the trees. Just before he vanished from sight, he stopped and looked back at Xavier over his shoulder. "I assume you won't have any trouble finding me with that nose of yours."

Then he was gone, his last statement confirming that he knew way more than he should.

For a moment, Xavier considered ignoring him completely. Only one person in his life had ever been allowed to give him orders, and it wasn't Colby. However, a soft sigh and the rustle of bed sheets behind him reminded him that he had someone else to think about now, another life he was responsible for. It wasn't what he was used to, but it was his new normal. He needed to make sure that Madelyn stayed safe.

Turning away from the window, Xavier moved for the bedroom door, snatching his pants off the ground as he went. Colby was right; it was time to end this once and for all.

The chilly night air hit his warm skin as he stepped out onto the porch, closing the door behind him with a soft click. He hadn't bothered with a shirt or shoes and socks because he didn't expect this to take very long. He may not know exactly what Colby had planned or how many guys waited for him in the cover of the trees, but he knew that he would be able to handle it quickly. Then, he would be back in bed before Madelyn even knew he was gone.

Xavier shoved his hands into his pockets as he made his way through the woods, leaves and twigs crunching beneath his bare feet. The further in he went, the more scents he began to catch on to that were mixing with Colby's. His original assessment had been correct; Colby hadn't come alone, which explained why he was being so bold. He didn't want to appear weak and afraid in front of the others. It didn't matter to Xavier either way though as he would take out as many of them as was necessary. Colby was still underestimating him if he believed a few more bodies were going to tip the odds in his favor.

In a matter of minutes, Xavier reached the small clearing. The cover of trees opened up to reveal a beautiful, cloudless sky, and moonlight was illuminating the area, not that he needed it. Colby stood at the other end, flanked by two guys he remembered from when he worked for Rodrigo. However, they had been so low on the totem pole that he hadn't bothered to learn their names, and he wasn't about to try now. They would be dead soon enough, along with Colby.

"You are like a cockroach, Colby," he commented casually, coming to a stop just inside the clearing. "You just don't go away."

"And you are surprisingly cocky for someone who's outnumbered," Colby stated, motioning to the two guys behind him.

Xavier smirked. "Three against one. I'd say the odds are still in my favor."

He knew there were way more than just the three men in front of him as he had scented at least fifteen more on the way here. He couldn't tell how many there were for sure because they were all grouped together and he hadn't had the time to pinpoint each individual scent. Though, Colby didn't need to know that he knew that. He wanted the guy to think he had the upper hand. And judging by the look on his face, he did.

Colby casually grasped his hands behind him as he began pacing. "Yeah, about that. I guess some of the guys were a bit upset that you had kept such a huge secret from all of us."

Xavier chuckled in response. "And I bet you were just all too happy to fill them in."

"Well, we are a family, after all. And families confide in each other. They had a right to know there was a monster in their midst. We all did."

"We are all monsters, Colby. I'm not special."

Freezing in place, Colby looked over at him and raised an eyebrow. "Well, now you are just being coy."

Xavier rolled his eyes. He was already bored with all of this. It was taking too long, and there was somewhere else he'd rather be, with someone far more interesting than the asshole before him.

"Are we going to do this, or what?" he asked impatiently. "Because I'm getting sick of listening to you talk."

Colby and the other two guys laughed, which wasn't the reaction he had been expecting. "Are you really that eager to die, Xavier?"

"You seem so sure you are going to win," he replied. "You know what I am, Colby, even with these two and all the others you have cowering in the trees, my death isn't guaranteed. However, what is a guarantee is the fact that more than a few of *you* will be dying tonight."

As he finished speaking, Xavier shifted on the spot, shredding through his sweatpants with his new form. He would have to walk back to the house naked now, but he didn't care. He was done with this shit.

After shaking out his fur, he looked up at the men in front of him. While Colby appeared unphased, having seen him shift before, the other two looked like they were about to crap their pants, which pleased him to no end.

With a low growl, he crouched low to the ground, making his intentions clear. Colby caught on and dove out of the way at the last minute as Xavier lunged forward. His claws pierced the chest of the first guy within seconds, and he had his throat torn out before they even hit the ground.

Spitting the blood and flesh from his mouth, he turned to the next guy. As much as he would have enjoyed dragging this out for as long as possible, making them suffer horribly, he couldn't afford to waste any time. Not when he was so outnumbered. He needed to end this.

The second guy was killed just as quickly as the first, and then his attention was on Colby, hoping to end this before it even began. He snarled and snapped at him, taking a few steps in Colby's direction. However, he was so enthralled by the scent of his fear that the three loud pops that came from the cover of the trees didn't even register until he felt the sharp pain in his flank.

Xavier spun around to see three large tranquilizer darts sticking out of his fur. It wasn't enough to knock him out, not with his rapid metabolism, but it was enough to drastically weaken him. He had underestimated Colby, had underestimated how much he knew about his kind, and he had expected him to still follow the rules set about by Rodrigo even though Isabelle had tried to warn him that he didn't. That was on him, and now he was paying for it.

As the tranquilizer coursed through his system, he growled at Colby, his steps stumbling before his legs gave out completely, and he crashed to the ground in a heap. Colby laughed again, the scabbed wound on the side of his face pinching as he closed the distance between the two of them. It was a stupid move on his part because everyone knew not to approach a cornered animal. Despite his rapidly weakening strength, Xavier was determined to make him pay for this.

The bastard even had the nerve to gently pat Xavier's cheek. "Don't worry, Xavier. We aren't going to kill you. Not yet anyway. Me and the guys?" He motioned toward the treeline.

Xavier blinked, trying to clear his blurring vision, and watched as about twenty men stepped out into the clearing, all former members of the family. Some of them he knew; most he didn't, but a few of them he had even considered a little more than acquaintances. Now though, they were all traitors in the eyes of Rodrigo.

"We have several years of pent-up frustration to get out," Colby continued.

Xavier growled and used every last ounce of his strength to claw Colby's face, right along the healing wounds from his previous attack. His claws tore at the flesh, feeling it rip and tear and open anew. Blood spilled down Colby's face as he screeched in agony. For several moments, no one in the clearing moved or even dared breathe.

Colby covered the side of his face with his hand, trying to stem the bleeding. He rose to his feet and then kicked Xavier square in the ribs, knocking the wind out of him and cracking two of his ribs in the process. "We are going to take our fucking time with you, freak," he spat angrily. "I hope you are ready because this is really going to fucking hurt!"

Colby backed away, ripping his shirt over his head to press the cloth against his face, and the first group of guys stepped forward. A man named Keith was the first to strike, a swift and hard kick in the same place Colby had kicked him just moments before. His ribs snapped under the force of the blow, and he roared in pain.

The beating began in full force then, each guy taking the opportunity to either punch or kick him. One even dislocated his hip joint, and there was nothing he could do to stop it, thanks to the sedative. He almost wished it had been enough to knock him out. While he had inflicted more than enough pain on others, being on the receiving end was a different thing entirely.

After what felt like an eternity of being beaten, having bones broken, tufts of fur yanked out, and being stabbed by various objects, the guys finally began to back away. Blood filled his mouth, and his body throbbed painfully. He blinked the one eye that wasn't swollen shut and watched as Colby stepped up next to him, twirling a metal bat in his hands. He smirked at Xavier, a look of triumph on his face.

"Not bad for the first round," he sneered. "And when you come to, we will do this all over again. This time, I win, Xavier."

Colby raised the bat over his head and brought it down with enough force to kill him had he been human. The bat cracked against his skull, but he mercifully blacked out before the pain of the blow could register, and he welcomed the darkness with open arms.

Chapter Seventeen
TWO WEEKS LATER

Madelyn

Madelyn hated to admit it, but she was depressed. Not to mention pissed. She had fallen asleep in Xavier's arms, exhausted from the intense but incredible sex, with him making promises of forever, only to wake up the next morning alone with his side of the bed cold and empty. That had been two weeks ago, and she hadn't seen or heard from him since. His bag was still sitting on the bay window, and the only things missing were his keys and his phone. Naturally, she was starting to think that everything he had said to her was a goddamn lie, and it hurt more than she cared to admit.

Despite her better judgment. She had fallen for the guy. His dirty mouth and the depraved games they had played had become a staple in her life, and she didn't know what to do without them anymore. She didn't know what to do without *him*. He wasn't even watching her from the shadows anymore because she was once again back to feeling completely and utterly alone. It was suffocating and damn near debilitating.

The only thing she could do was try to keep herself busy to keep her mind off of the soul-sucking darkness that threatened to consume her. Staying busy meant that she couldn't get lost in the dark depths of her mind. She wouldn't get stuck trying to figure out what she did wrong to make Xavier leave her the way he did. Focusing on how angry she was at him helped, as did the fact that she was seemingly fighting off a really bad cold.

A couple of days ago, she woke up feeling like she had been hit by a dump truck. She was nauseated and dizzy and was having a hard time keeping anything down. She had thought it would have gone away or at least started to ease up a bit, but it was staying steady. So, after throwing up for the third time that morning, she made a call to her doctor to set an appointment. Thankfully, she managed to squeeze her in for later that afternoon.

Madelyn was sitting on the couch in a shirt and sweats, waiting for Bernie to show up to take her to the clinic. She didn't trust herself to drive as lightheaded as she was feeling, and she couldn't call Melanie since the two of them still weren't talking. In hindsight, she still couldn't believe she had blown up an amazing friendship for a guy who just ghosted her once he got what he wanted from her.

A part of her wondered if maybe it was the chase that had kept him interested. Maybe he only wanted her when he couldn't have her, and it pissed her off that she had fallen for it too. She was furious in fact and wanted nothing more than to give Xavier a piece of her mind. It was that desire that had her texting and calling him a couple of times a day and had her pulling up his number again now.

Once again, the phone just continued to ring over and over again, only fueling her frustration further. She growled and was just about to hang up when she suddenly heard the distinct sound of someone picking up and sighing heavily.

"Yeah."

Madelyn blinked and glanced at the phone to see if she accidentally misdialed. She knew Xavier's voice as well as she knew her own, and the voice that answered was unmistakably female.

"Hello?" the voice pressed, sounding irritated.

"Uh, I'm sorry. I was looking for Xavier?" she stammered.

"He's… unavailable at the moment. Who is this?"

"Madelyn."

Her answer was instinctive as her mind was still trying to process what was going on. Everything Xavier had said to her had been a lie to get into her pants, it had to be. She wasn't his mate or soulmate, or whatever. It had all been a way for him to get her into bed and he had obviously moved on already. However, why he had left his duffel bag with some of his clothes and some other interesting toys behind was still a mystery to her. Not that it mattered. She should have known better than to give in to him, and she should have listened to Melanie from the very beginning. She should have turned the prick in to the police when she had the chance.

"Madelyn? Oh, yeah. I've heard about you."

"Uh-huh. And who are you?" she countered, not sure she wanted to know the answer.

"Oh, I'm Isabelle. I'm a… *friend* of Xavier's."

Her stomach soured in an instant, bile rising in her throat. Xavier had admitted that he and Isabelle had a history, a *sexual* history. It had been yet another lie when he told her that she didn't have anything to worry about when it came to Isabelle because he had run right back to her once he was done with her. How could she have been so stupid?

"Listen, Madelyn. There's something you should know," Isabelle began, her voice softening. "About Xavier."

"No, I think I know enough," she snapped quickly. "Sorry I bothered you."

Without giving Isabelle the chance to respond, she ended the call and immediately blocked Xavier's number. She was done with him. She had to be for her own sanity.

Xavier was a walking red flag, and yet she had ignored all the signs. She had embraced him and his darkness even though a part of her had known it was going to end this way. She had even allowed herself to develop feelings for him, to lose herself in him, and now she was paying the price. She had no one to blame but herself.

The tears in her eyes began to fall more freely now, her chest feeling like it had been cut open and was spilling all over the floor. As hard as it was though, she decided to let herself feel it this time instead of forcing it down. If she allowed herself to feel this pain, if she embraced it for a while, then she would be less inclined to make the same mistake again. Reaching over to the edge of the couch, she grabbed the navy blue sweatshirt of Xavier's that she had been basically living in the last couple of days.

A soft sob escaped her lips as she pulled it over her head. At the same time, there was a knock on her door. As always, Bernie was right on time. Wiping her face, she pushed herself off the couch and made her way toward the door, grabbing her purse on the way out.

"Hey, kiddo," Bernie greeted with a smile once she opened the door. "You ready to go?"

"Hey, Bernie. Yeah, I'm ready."

She stepped out onto the porch and locked the door behind her before Bernie took her arm and led her to the car. It was an old beat-up station wagon that smelled like leather polish and cigars. It fit Bernie perfectly.

"Thanks for doing this, Bernie," she said as they pulled out onto the road. "I appreciate it."

He glanced over at her, still beaming. "Of course! Happy to do it. Though, I am surprised that you didn't ask Melanie. Is… is everything alright between the two of you?"

Madelyn turned her gaze out of the passenger side window, worried that she might start crying again. "Why do you ask?"

She felt rather than saw him shrug. "Like I said, usually, you'd ask Melanie to take you to your appointments. Don't get me wrong. I really am happy to do it. I just thought she'd be far better company. Not to mention the fact that you look like crap."

"Hey!" she exclaimed with a small, weak laugh. "I look like crap because I'm sick."

"Maybe that's part of it, but I know you well enough to know that there's something else going on with you too," he replied. "You can't hide that shit from a seasoned detective. Add to that the fact that Melanie has been just as depressed and has snapped at everyone at the station more than a few times, and it's easy to put two and two together. Did you guys get into a fight or something?"

It didn't bring her any form of joy knowing that Melanie was seemingly suffering too. In fact, she hated it because it was all her fault.

She chewed on her cheek, trying to keep the emotion from her voice. "Not a fight so much as a very big disagreement. It's not like we started throwing fists or anything."

"Well, what was the disagreement about? Anything I

can do to help? I do have a wealth of knowledge, you know."

"I appreciate that," she said truthfully. "But I don't think there's anything anyone can do. Melanie made it clear that she's done with me."

"Well now. I don't believe that for a second."

Madelyn looked over at him and lifted an eyebrow in question.

Bernie just shrugged again, not taking his eyes off the road. "Come on. I've seen the two of you together. You guys are like sisters. And sisters fight all the time. I have little doubt that the two of you will work it out in no time."

That was one of the things Madelyn loved about Bernie. He had one of the biggest hearts of anyone she knew, and he had the kind of optimism that was contagious. It managed to ignite a small spark of hope within her chest despite her attempts to squash it back down. She wanted nothing more than to believe that she and Melanie could reconcile and go back to the way things were before she had let a man come between them.

However, Madelyn was worried about getting her hopes up. A part of her knew that the chances of that were slim. After everything she had done when it came to Xavier, she didn't blame Melanie either.

A gentle pat on her leg from Bernie pulled her out of her thoughts. She glanced up at him to see him looking at her expectantly. Apparently, he had attempted to continue the conversation but she had been too lost in her own mind to realize it.

She shook herself mentally. "What? Sorry."

"Nothing. Nevermind." He paused for a moment before a small smile spread across his lips. "So, you got a new man in your life yet?"

Madelyn couldn't help but laugh. Not only because of

the sudden change in topic but also because of the irony behind his question. If only he knew how closely the two topics were related.

Chapter Eighteen

Madelyn

*P*regnant.

As much as she didn't want to believe it, that was what the test results she held in her hand said clear as day. That and she was mildly anemic. Either way, it explained why she had felt like such crap these last few days. She was pregnant, and only one guy could be the father. It just didn't make any sense. It shouldn't have been possible.

When she had come into the clinic and told them about her symptoms, they had insisted on running a whole battery of tests, 'just to be safe'. Vitals, blood, urine—they had done it all. While she didn't know what she had expected; cold, flu, stomach bug, she didn't once even consider that this might be the cause.

"I don't understand," she said softly, unable to look away from the one word on the page that was changing her entire life. "I'm on birth control. I've been on birth control since I was a teenager. How is this—"

"It happens sometimes," Dr. Price replied, the tone of her voice implying that it was not a big deal. "It's rare, but it happens. I'm guessing this isn't what you expected when you came in today?"

Madelyn scoffed a laugh and shook her head. "No. This was definitely *not* on my bingo card."

She had heard stories about it happening before, women getting pregnant while on birth control, but they had been so few and far between that she never thought it would happen to her. To top it off, it could not have happened with the worst possible man.

Xavier was a murderer. He had admitted to killing countless people, and he'd stalked her for months. Unhinged didn't even begin to describe the guy, and then there was the fact that he was a shifter. What did all of that mean for the tiny life that was now growing inside of her?

Because she didn't know very much about shifters, she wasn't sure how she was supposed to raise one. It wasn't like there were any baby books on the subject, and Xavier was out of the picture since she had no intention of telling him about the baby. Why would she? She wasn't the kind of girl to try to trap a guy by getting pregnant, and he had moved on already anyway.

"I'm going to set up a referral for you to see Dr. Catherine Diaz," Dr. Price continued, making a few notes in her file. "She's an amazing OBGyn and a very good friend of mine. She can tell you how far along you are and go over the next steps. You will be in good hands with her."

"Thanks," she muttered, deciding not to comment on the fact that she already knew how far along she was. She may not know which time he had knocked her up, but she still had a fairly good idea.

She also knew what the next steps would be as well. Months of morning sickness, weird cravings, weight gain, and that was if she decided to keep it. That was something she was going to have to figure out sooner rather than later. She doubted that she was capable of handling being a single mother to a shifter child, but she didn't think she would ever forgive herself if she got rid of it. It was not the kind of decision that could be taken lightly; it was one that required a lot of thought.

Madelyn ran her fingers through her hair, unable to believe that she was in this position in the first place.

Dr. Price seemed to be oblivious to the downward spiral that was going on in her mind. "In the meantime, I'll prescribe some prenatal vitamins and anti-nausea meds. They should help give you some relief and allow you to get some food in you."

Nodding, Madelyn cleared her throat. She couldn't freak out, not yet. She could at least wait until she got home before she lost it. "Thank you, Dr. Price. I appreciate it."

The doctor patted her leg in response. "Chin up, Madelyn. This is supposed to be the happiest time in your life, becoming a mother. Once the shock wears off, you will see that."

She highly doubted that.

Rising to her feet, Dr. Price picked up the file and headed to the door. Just before she opened it, she looked back at Madelyn from over her shoulder and smiled. "You are good to go. You can get dressed. I'll go put in the referral and the prescriptions. Take care of yourself, Madelyn, and take it easy the next few days. At least until you regain some of your strength."

"Okay, will do," Madelyn replied, jumping off the exam table. She was more than ready to get out of there because she was in desperate need of some fresh air. The room was beginning to feel stuffy and small.

"Oh, and congratulations, mama." With that and a wink, the doctor vanished down the hall, leaving Madelyn staring after her.

Madelyn managed to dress herself in a kind of daze. Her mind was still reeling from the news she had received, and she was still having trouble believing it even though the proof was right in front of her. She kept looking at the test results, thinking they had made a mistake somehow. But every time she looked, it only drove the fact home.

After getting rid of the scratchy hospital gown and changing back into her own clothes, Madelyn picked up her purse and then made her way to the pharmacy counter. The clinic must not have been that busy because they handed her a small white bag with her medications as soon as she showed them her ID. Madelyn shoved the bag into her purse before wandering into the waiting room where Bernie was still waiting for her.

He jumped up as she approached and looked her up and down expectantly. "Well?" he asked as she led him quickly out of the building. She couldn't seem to get outside fast enough. "Did they figure out what's going on with you?"

"Uh, yeah," she replied. "Yeah, they did."

There was always the option to lie to him. She could say that it was just a cold and that she was fine, but she was just so sick of all the lies. She didn't want to do it anymore, nor did she have the strength to keep them all straight. So, at that moment, she decided that the truth was all she had.

Bernie laughed when she didn't say anything more and gently grasped her arm just before she stepped into the parking lot. "Well? Do I need to start planning your funeral, or are you going to get better soon?"

"Um, define soon. Because what I have usually sticks around for about nine months or so. Plus side though, I'm fairly certain it won't kill me." She wasn't trying to make light of the situation. It wasn't anything to laugh at, but humor was her defense mechanism, and she was feeling rather defensive.

Bernie, however, didn't laugh. He just stared at her in surprise. "You're… you're pregnant?"

"Yup."

Madelyn went to step around him to go back to the car, but Bernie was in front of her again. "Hang on. You just told me on the way here that there wasn't a man in your life. Are you holding out on me, kiddo?"

Laughing softly, she shook her head. "No, I'm not holding out on you, Bernie. There is no man in my life. I thought there might be for a bit, but it didn't work out."

The two started walking again, crossing the parking lot together. "Are you going to tell him? About the baby?"

"Honestly, I'm not sure," she admitted. "I haven't seen or spoken to him in two weeks, and another girl answered when I called him this morning. A girl he previously admitted to having a sexual relationship with. So, I'm pretty sure he's done with me."

"You're joking," Bernie deadpanned.

"Oh, I wish I was joking. That would make the fact that I'm pregnant a little easier to swallow."

Taking her arm, Bernie weaved it through his and pulled her close. "Do you want me to kill him? Because I've been a cop a long time. I can do it and easily get away with it. I know what to watch out for."

At that, Madelyn laughed harder than she had in the last several days. It felt odd, foreign considering all she was going through, but she had needed it. It provided a hint of reprieve from the darkness threatening to consume her whole.

"I'm sure you could, but that's not necessary."

"There she is," he commented. When they finally reached the car, she turned and looked up at him. He poked her nose with a smile. "I missed that pretty smile of yours. In all seriousness though, Madelyn, you are going to be a wonderful mother."

Color flooded her cheeks as she averted her gaze to the ground. "That's very kind of you to say, Bernie, but I'm not too sure about that. My parents—"

"Hey, I'm not talking about *your* parents. I'm talking about you. I know what kind of person you are, and despite what you've been through in your past, you have one of the biggest hearts of anyone I know. And I—"

All of a sudden, a big black van skidded to a stop in front of them where they were standing next to Bernie's station wagon, cutting off whatever Bernie was about to say. As the back door of the van flew open, Bernie shoved her behind him protectively, but then she heard a strange popping sound, and Madelyn found herself splattered with warm, sticky blood. Bernie's blood.

Everything happened so fast that she didn't even have the chance to scream. All she could do was stare stupidly at the gaping hole in the back of Bernie's head. She realized that she was looking at parts of his skull and brain too. She had seen much worse on TV and in movies, but it was somehow vastly different when seen in person.

It seemed to take his body a few moments to catch up to the fact that he was dead too. Then, when his body finally collapsed onto the pavement at her feet, Madelyn found herself facing none other than Colby, the guy who was after Xavier, and the gun he had just used to kill her friend.

Lowering said gun, Colby smirked at her, pinching the claw marks that ran down the side of his face, which Xavier had given him the day she found out what Xavier was. Half of Colby's face was scarred now, and it also looked to be infected.

"Hello again, Madelyn. Long time no see."

"What did you do?" she gasped, her eyes filling with tears.

Two guys grabbed her arms, her purse clattering to the ground next to Bernie's body, and they began pulling her toward the open back door of the van.

"What did you do?" she screamed again, struggling against the guys' grasp. "What did you do?"

"What I had to," Colby told her as they passed.

The guys tossed her unceremoniously into the back of the van and climbed in after her to hold her down. Colby climbed in last, closing the door behind them. Within seconds, they were speeding off. The whole ordeal felt like it had taken forever when it had happened within a matter of seconds.

One of the guys zip-tied Madelyn's hands together while the other did the same to her ankles after she had kicked him in his face. Colby just sat there, his back resting against the back of the passenger seat, watching the scene unfold.

A gag was placed over her mouth, though it wasn't necessary. Whether it was the shock of watching Bernie die so suddenly or the knowledge that she was being kidnapped by trained assassins, Madelyn had given up. She stopped struggling and trying to scream for help because both were just a waste of energy.

Bernie was dead. One minute, he was saying the nicest things to her, things a father should have said, and the next, he was gone. His life had been stolen by a man who had come for her. She just wished she knew why.

"We're clear, boss," the man behind the wheel said after a while. "No one's following."

"Good, take us back to camp then," Colby replied, tapping his gun on the side of his knee while not taking his eyes off of her. "I'm sorry about your friend, Madelyn. Collateral damage, you understand. Just like you, I'm afraid. Since I'm unable to reach Xavier myself, I have to be able to draw him out somehow. What better way to do that than by using the woman he loves, right?"

Madelyn didn't even give him the satisfaction of acknowledging that he'd spoken to her. She didn't even look at him. What was the point? It wasn't like it would change anything even if he believed the fact that his plan wasn't going to work. He would probably kill her on principle. He had said it before; no witnesses.

To Colby, she wasn't a person right now. She wasn't a human being with feelings or emotions, nor was she a broken woman who just found out she was pregnant with her stalker's baby. To him, she was just a tool, a way for him to get what he wanted. However, once he realized that using her wasn't going to get him any closer to Xavier, she wouldn't even be that anymore. She would just be a liability. There was no way she was getting out of this. She knew that now. Death was imminent, for both her and her baby.

Chapter Nineteen

Xavier

The first thing he noticed as he began to regain consciousness was the silence. It was too quiet, especially with as many guys as Colby had with him. He knew enough about these guys to know that they were only ever quiet while on a job, and this wasn't a job. Not a sanctioned one anyway. Rodrigo's place had never been this quiet because, when guys like them got together in one place, fights were inevitable.

The next thing he noticed was the intense and excruciating pain, causing him to take account of his injuries. It felt as though every bone in his body had been shattered and was slowly fusing themselves back together, particularly in his head. It had been a very long time since he'd felt pain this severe, but he would heal. He had done it before and was clearly doing so now.

It took him a few moments, but he managed to pry both of his eyes open. They felt like sandpaper, and one was still swollen, but his shifter healing was seemingly working overtime. The last he remembered, he couldn't open one eye at all.

Xavier blinked against the brightness of the room, willing his eyes to adjust as quickly as possible. He needed to figure out where they were holding him so that he could come up with a plan. However, he wasn't expecting to discover that he was in his own room. Nor did he expect to see the familiar head of red hair standing over by the window.

"Isabelle?" he croaked, his throat hoarse and sore.

Isabelle turned from the window and gave him a bright smile as she crossed the room. She sat on the edge of the bed. "Hey, stranger. Welcome back."

She reached forward and brushed a strand of hair from his forehead, causing his wolf to snarl at her boldness. He was still a bit feral and felt cornered due to the extent of his injuries.

"Don't," he warned with a growl.

If she heard him, she didn't let on. "We thought we were going to lose you there for a bit. Thank God for that freaky healing ability of yours."

"I thought you didn't believe in God," he quipped back.

"It's a figure of speech, Xavier. Don't be an ass."

Xavier winced as he shifted, trying to get into a more comfortable position. "How did I get here? And where is Colby?"

Isabelle sighed and ran a perfectly manicured finger through her hair. "We don't know where he is," she admitted. "We managed to track you guys down because Rodrigo told us where you'd most likely be. We got there just in time to see Colby take a bat to that big-ass dome of yours. We got as many as we could, but most of them got away. Colby included. And they seemed to have gone underground too. Since they know how we track people, they know how to stay under the radar. But we will find him. It's just going to take a little more time."

Xavier blinked. "A little more time? Isabelle, how long was I out?"

"About two weeks," she said with a shrug as if it was no big deal.

But it was a big deal, a very big deal. Madelyn had been alone and unprotected for two whole weeks with Colby still out there. Colby was the only person, apart from Rodrigo, who knew how important she was to him. If he was going to do something to get to him, going after Madelyn was the most logical choice.

Gritting his teeth to keep himself from roaring in pain, Xavier pushed himself out of bed. He needed to find his phone, and then he needed to get back to Madelyn's place. Both he and his wolf needed to make sure that she was okay. It was the only thing he could think about, the only thing going through his mind.

"Whoa, hey!" Isabelle suddenly exclaimed, rushing around to his side of the bed to try to push him back down. "You can't be up and walking right now."

He snarled at her when she tried to touch his arm. It didn't go unnoticed that he was still very naked, and no one was allowed to touch him but Madelyn. No one.

"Back off, Isabelle. I have to get out of here."

Isabelle blinked at him in surprise but recovered quickly. "No, you need to focus on healing. You can't take on Colby like this, shifter or not. Besides, we don't even know where he is."

Pain coursed through his entire body as he limped his way to his dresser to grab some clothes. "I'm not going after Colby," he hissed through his teeth. "I'm going to get Madelyn. I have to protect her."

"Your fucking booty call?" Isabelle exclaimed, rolling her eyes. "Jesus Christ, Xavier. Now is not the time to—"

Xavier was on her before he realized what he was doing. His eyes were blazing, and he had Isabelle pinned to the wall by her throat, his claws piercing the soft flesh of her neck until tiny beads of blood rolled down her neck.

It would be so easy to puncture her carotid or snap her neck for saying such a thing about his mate. He could end her life in an instant, and she seemed to have enough sense to realize that too as her eyes widened and her body went still. He could smell the acrid stench of her fear permeating the air around them, and it fueled him further.

"I am only going to say this once, Isabelle. You watch your fucking mouth when you talk about Madelyn. Friend or not, I won't hesitate to kill you if you disrespect her like that in front of me again. You got it?"

Isabelle nodded quickly. "Y-yeah. Yeah, I got it."

Retracting his claws from her skin, he pushed himself away from her and moved back to the dresser. He dressed quickly while Isabelle rubbed her neck behind him. But he couldn't be bothered with her right now, not when there was something more important he needed to do. Once he was dressed, he stormed from the room as quickly as was possible in his current condition, and Isabelle wasn't too far behind him.

Xavier found his cell phone charging on the kitchen island and snatched it up. He pulled up Madelyn's number and punched the call button. When the call just continued to ring, he realized that she must have blocked him. It didn't surprise him since he essentially ghosted her for two weeks, but it pissed him off too. While she may be pissed at him, she had just made it impossible for him to explain and to check on her. His disappearance had not been his choice, and he had thought that she would have realized that. Apparently, he had been wrong.

Moving to the bedroom, he flipped on the switch that awakened his computer system. He winced as he took a seat in the chair and pulled up the cameras at Madelyn's place. It didn't take long to figure out she wasn't at home, even though the tracker on her car had it parked in the driveway. And after a quick scan of the station's cameras, to see if she had cut her leave short and gotten a ride into work, he discovered she wasn't there either. He growled in frustration and slammed his hand down on the desk, sending another wave of pain shooting up his arm.

"She called yesterday, you know," Isabelle said softly, causing him to turn around. She was leaning against the doorway, still rubbing her neck and clearly trying to keep her distance. Good. "She called a lot while you were out, in fact. It was kind of annoying."

His eyes narrowed dangerously as he slowly rose to his feet. "What did you do, Isabelle?"

"Nothing, I swear. I answered the phone and had every intention of telling her that you were hurt, but she hung up before I got the chance."

His jaw clenched as he struggled to maintain his composure. He had a pretty good idea *why* she had hung up on Isabelle like that, and that just pissed him off even more. Madelyn probably assumed he had gone back to Isabelle, even though he had never given her any reason to doubt him.

Turning back to the computer screen, he sat down and began doing what he usually did when he was looking for someone; he started a search. He began searching for any activity on her credit cards and checking hotel records to see if she had checked in somewhere. However, he was surprised when he got a hit from the Cedarwood Police Department.

According to the report, Madelyn had been labeled as 'missing' after she had disappeared from the parking lot of the local medical clinic yesterday afternoon. Her purse and cell phone were found next to the dead body of CPD Detective Bernie Slopes, who was killed by a single gunshot wound to the head. It was quick, clean, and there were no witnesses.

"Colby," he sneered, rage bubbling in his chest as his vision became tinged with red.

"What?" Isabelle asked curiously.

Xavier glanced at who the lead detective was on the case and rolled his eyes before he rose from his seat. The anger, fear, and adrenaline were masking the pain from his injuries, which was good. He was going to need every ounce of strength he had to get through what he had to do.

"Colby has Madelyn," he stated, scrolling through his phone and exiting the room.

Once again, Isabelle was behind him. "Oh, come on, Xavier. You don't know that."

"Yeah, I do." He smashed his finger against the call button on his phone again and brought it to his ear. "Unlike you, Colby understands how important she is to me. And since he hasn't been able to get to me, going after Madelyn is the next best thing."

There was a click on the other end of the phone before a familiar but unwelcome voice filled his ear. "Hello?"

"Melanie," he ground out, grabbing his keys and stuff off the entry table and heading out the front door with Isabelle on his heels. "We need to talk. I know who has Madelyn."

He was taking a huge risk, going to Melanie, but he

didn't have any other option. He needed to know what she knew and what leads, if any, she had. He also needed to warn her because, when he found Madelyn, and he *would* find her, she was going to need her best friend. Melanie couldn't go after Colby, but he could. It didn't matter what happened to him as long as Madelyn was safe.

Chapter Twenty

Xavier

"You must still have some serious brain damage if you think that this is a good fucking idea," Isabelle complained, pacing the concrete.

The two of them were standing in the parking lot of one of the buildings that was currently under construction and a few blocks from the station. When he made the call, it was under the assumption that Melanie still cared about Madelyn, and he had assumed correctly as it hadn't taken much to get her to agree to meet with him. She had been so eager for any shred of information that she hadn't even asked who he was, what information he had, or why he asked to meet with her alone. In truth, she was lucky it had been him who asked to meet with her instead of Colby or one of his guys.

"No one said you need to be here," he snapped at her.

"Obviously, I do need to be here," she retorted. "You

have kept what you are a secret for years, but the moment you leave us, all of a sudden you tell everyone who will listen! You are going to end up getting yourself killed!"

Isabelle was currently pushing every single one of his buttons, and he was seconds away from completely losing it on her. He didn't know why she cared so much. It wasn't like it was her secret he was exposing. Who he told had no impact on her or her life whatsoever.

Thankfully, he was saved from biting her head off by Melanie coming around the corner of the building. She looked exactly as he expected her to since her best friend was missing. Her hair was up in a messy bun, her clothes were wrinkled, and she was wearing day-old makeup. Madelyn's disappearance seemed to be weighing heavily on her.

Melanie's steps slowed when she spotted both him and Isabelle, and her hand instinctively went to the gun on her belt. "Are you the one who called? The one with information about Madelyn?"

"I am," he replied, folding his arms across his chest.

"Right," she muttered as she eyed him skeptically. "And how did you come about this information? Were you in the parking lot when it happened, or—"

He raised an eyebrow in question. "You are asking those questions now?"

Melanie rolled her eyes and threw her arms out in clear frustration. "I don't have time for this."

"Melanie, I know who took Madelyn because he's after me. He knows how much hurting Madelyn would hurt me," he said quickly.

Shifting on her feet, Melanie's eyes narrowed as she took him in. "You're him," she said after a while. "You're Xavier. Madelyn's stalker."

"Boyfriend," he corrected impatiently. "I was upgraded."

"I should arrest your ass where you stand."

"For what, exactly? Last I checked, you've got nothing on me."

Melanie lifted her chin defiantly. "Don't I? What about what you did to David?"

The corner of his mouth twitched up despite the current situation. That was a memory he was rather fond of. Melanie was smart, he'd give her that. She knew what he had done to David, but if he had ID'd him, he would be in cuffs already. As it stood, she was bluffing.

"Who's David?" he asked nonchalantly.

"I thought you two were here to talk about Madelyn," Isabelle interjected impatiently. "Isn't she missing or some shit?"

"And who the fuck are you?" The accusation was clear in Melanie's voice as she glared at Isabelle before looking back at him. "Are you screwing her too? Does Madelyn know?"

He didn't have time for this shit. Madelyn was out there somewhere, in Colby's hands, no less. He needed to get this moving along.

"Isabelle is an old associate of mine, and yes, Madelyn knows about her. Madelyn knows more about me than you think." Melanie cocked an eyebrow in question, but he continued. "So, here's the deal. The man who killed your guy? His name is Colby, and you do *not* want to go after him, okay? You will only get yourself and anyone you take with you killed."

Melanie laughed humorlessly. "You are a real piece of work, you know that? I don't know what Madelyn even sees in you. I *am* going to find her, Xavier. Not only is it my job, but unlike you, I'm not going to leave her with some psycho."

"Damn it, Melanie!" he exclaimed loudly. "I'm not leaving her with Colby. I'm going after him."

"And you are better suited to do so because?"

Taking a step toward her, he was about to tell her, but Isabelle surprisingly beat him to it. "Because we are hired killers, Detective. We were all trained by the same man from a very young age. We know how Colby works and operates, and we know how to take him down."

He found it shocking that Isabelle had divulged so much. It wasn't like her, but at least, she was helping to keep the conversation going.

"I was higher up in the chain of command than Colby was," he continued, motioning toward his still-healing face. "And he still managed to take me down. That's why Madelyn was taken. I was unconscious for the last two weeks. If I hadn't been, then I would have protected her. But I'm ready for him this time, and you have my word that I will get Madelyn back. But you can't go after him, Melanie. You will only get yourself killed."

The look on Melanie's face was one of disbelief. "You… you came here to warn me? To protect me?"

"Trust me, I can't believe it either. This shit isn't what I do, but when I found out that you were leading the investigation, I had to warn you, for Madelyn's sake. And now I have. So—"

Xavier nodded at Isabelle, letting her know, without words, that they were leaving. However, Melanie's voice stopped him. "Why?" she asked suddenly. When he looked over at her, she continued. "Why bother to warn me? Why do you care what happens to me? Surely, you know by now that I have never been supportive of whatever fucked up relationship you have with Madelyn."

"I'm aware," he stated simply as he turned to face her once more. "And to be frank, I couldn't give two shits about what happens to you. But you are important to Madelyn. You are her best friend. If anything happens to you, it will devastate her, and I'd like to avoid that if possible."

"You really do care about her." It was Isabelle who spoke, but he didn't take his eyes off Melanie.

"I love her."

Those three simple words felt strange on his tongue. He had never said them out loud to anyone since his mother died. Once she died, he had vowed to never say them again. However, meeting Madelyn had changed everything.

Melanie sighed heavily. "Okay, look. I may not understand this whole thing between you two, and to be honest, I may never understand it, but I can tell that you mean that."

"I do." And he had never meant anything more.

"And I could tell that Madelyn cares about you too when she was telling me about the two of you."

"What's your point, Melanie?" he asked impatiently.

"My point is it would devastate Madelyn if anything happened to you, too, and this guy already bested you once."

Xavier shook his head and did something that he had never done before. He gently grasped Melanie's arms in his hands. "Again, that was just because I underestimated him and was vastly outnumbered. I won't make that mistake again. Trust me."

Melanie shifted on her feet and rolled her eyes. "I care about her too, you know. Like you said, she's my best friend. So, forgive me if I can't take someone like you at your word."

He should have just left it at that. He had already spent more time there than he had planned to, but he had to do something. Otherwise, Melanie wasn't going to listen to him. She would go after Colby and end up getting herself killed.

Taking a step away from her, he winced as he pulled off his sweatshirt. "I'm going to show you something, Melanie. Something that will explain how I can be so confident that I can take down Colby and how I know that Madelyn and I are destined to be together."

Melanie shook her head, confused. "What do you—"

"Just watch, Melanie," he interrupted harshly. "I don't have the time or the patience to explain it all in detail."

Melanie pressed her lips together as Xavier nodded at Isabelle, who moved closer to the good detective in case she needed to grab her. Considering the way the conversation had gone, he had hoped that he wouldn't have to go to these lengths. But he didn't see any way out of this. It might be the only way to convince Melanie to let him handle this.

Xavier cracked his neck and mentally prepared himself for the pain that was about to come. Usually, shifting wasn't painful, but he was still healing. He probably shouldn't be shifting at all due to his injuries, but it was probably better that he do so and get a feel for the kind of pain it was going to cause now rather than when he came face to face with the enemy. When Madelyn needed him.

Without giving himself the time to think, he ground his teeth together and shifted in the blink of an eye. It hurt like hell, but it was bearable, which was good to know. He chuffed and shook out his fur.

When he looked up at Melanie, her eyes were nearly bulging out of her face as she began to scramble for her gun. Isabelle stopped her by shoving her against the wall and clamping a hand over her mouth to keep her quiet.

"Perfect," she huffed, glaring at him in his wolf form as she fought to keep a hold on Melanie. "What now, Einstein?"

Chapter Twenty-One

Xavier

"Alright, just keep me posted," Melanie said into her phone before she ended the call and sat down in the chair he had brought into his office for her. She dropped the phone into her purse before leaning back against the chair. "They don't have any leads yet, but they will let me know if that changes."

Xavier only nodded as he began a new search parameter on his computer.

It hadn't been his intention to bring Melanie back to his place as he didn't want her involved in all this. That was why he had gone to see her and told her to back off in the first place. However, once the shock of discovering what he was had worn off, she insisted he bring her along and didn't give him much choice in the matter. She said that, if he didn't, she'd arrest him for obstruction, and even she seemed to know that his kind would not do well in county lockup.

The whole situation was awkward as hell because they despised each other. Their love for Madelyn was the only thing that was uniting them right now, and he wasn't going to be the one to make Madelyn choose between them. He knew how important Melanie was to her. So, he'd tolerate the pushy detective for Madelyn's sake, at least, for now.

"Is any of this even legal?" Melanie asked him pointedly as she stared at the screen from over his shoulder.

"You aren't here as a cop, remember? You don't get to sit here and question our methods, nor do you get to use anything you see or hear against us in any way. That was the deal."

He had already gone over all of this with her before he agreed to bring her here, but he also felt it was necessary to reinforce the issue.

Isabelle and the others Rodrigo had sent were in the living room, coming up with a plan of action for when he found out where Colby was hiding. Despite being told otherwise, they had decided to work together, and Melanie's presence had them all on edge. He wouldn't put it past any one of them, especially Isabelle, to kill her if they thought for one moment that she was a threat. This meant he also needed to keep an eye on her so that Madelyn didn't lose her best friend, another meaningless task that he wanted no part of.

"I am aware, Xavier," Melanie said. "But that doesn't mean I have to like this arrangement."

"What do you know—something we have in common," he grumbled in response.

After a few moments, she spoke again. "So, I'm guessing that Madelyn knows you are not human."

"She does."

"And she agreed to be with you anyway?" The way her voice held a hint of disgust pissed him off.

His jaw clenched in irritation. "Yes, because, unlike you, she's not a judgmental bitch."

"Hey, I'm not judging," she retorted, causing him to snort. "Okay, maybe I am a bit. But I just figured that someone like you would want to be with your own kind. Surely, another shifter could handle your… proclivities a bit better than a mere human can."

Xavier turned to face her then, his hands balling into fists so tightly that his claws punctured the flesh of his palm. He was really trying to keep his anger and irritation in check, but Melanie wasn't making it easy. If it were any other time, he wouldn't mind the questions, especially if it helped her to accept his place in Madelyn's life. But right now, Madelyn was in danger, and he needed to focus on finding her.

"Madelyn handles my proclivities just fine," he snapped. "And for your information, there are no female shifters. Even if there were, Madelyn is my fated mate. She's it for me."

Melanie's eyebrow lifted in question. "What the fuck does that mean?"

He debated not telling her as he didn't owe her a damn thing. He knew how she felt about him, and he wasn't exactly fond of her either, especially after she had hurt Madelyn so badly. But she was still important to Madelyn, and when he found her, she was going to need Melanie too. Even he could set aside his own pride enough to admit that.

"It means that she's my soulmate, my wolf's other half. We have a kind of bond that is impossible to ignore and impossible to break. It's hard to explain because it's a shifter thing, but before you even ask, she knows about that too."

"Well, I'd hope so," she muttered. "Jesus, that's a lot to unpack."

Xavier didn't respond. He didn't feel like he needed to. How well Melanie understood what was between him and Madelyn didn't matter. He had done his part and had told her what she needed to know. At least, that's what he thought.

"You and Madelyn had sex, didn't you?"

His head snapped in her direction, his brows furrowed. "How the fuck is that any of your business?"

Melanie pressed her lips together, her hands fidgeting in her lap. The change in her demeanor was a little jarring, even to him. "It's not," she replied.

"Alright then."

"Can… can you just answer the question, Xavier?"

"Yes!" he exclaimed loudly, slamming his fists on the desk. "Okay? Yes, I fucked her. Several times. Is that all you wanted to know, or do you want all the dirty details too?"

"God, no," she gasped. "I just… When was the last time you spoke to her?"

"Two weeks ago or so, why?"

If he was being honest, he didn't like the direction the conversation was going. There was something in her voice that told him that she wasn't asking sheerly out of morbid curiosity. There was a point to her questions.

Melanie nodded, seemingly to herself. "And how did she seem? Did she seem okay?"

"Melanie," he pressed. "What's going on?"

She sighed and leaned back in her chair. "Okay, you know Madelyn was at the clinic when she was taken."

He nodded impatiently.

"Well, we found her purse at the scene, and there were some… things in it."

"Okay," he stated hesitantly. "What kinds of 'things'?"

"I don't know if I should be the one to tell you, I mean, this is probably something that you should hear from Madelyn herself," Melanie muttered quickly. "I just thought that maybe she had said something to you about it since she didn't say anything to me."

"Well, she didn't. So, spit it out."

He could see how much it hurt her that Madelyn hadn't said anything to her, but her evasiveness around the whole thing was beginning to put him on edge. Melanie was making it sound like there was something *wrong* with Madelyn. If that was the case, then finding her was even more dire. Being in the hands of someone like Colby was bad enough for someone in perfect health, and it sounded as though Madelyn *wasn't* in perfect health.

He knew that Colby wouldn't kill her right away. He wanted to use her to get to him, and he couldn't do that if she were dead. But who knew what the guy was doing to her in the meantime? The thought didn't sit well with him.

"Melanie!" he snapped, making the frustrating woman before him jump. "What's wrong with Madelyn?"

"Nothing! Jesus." When he lifted an eyebrow, she rolled her eyes. "I'm serious, Xavier. Nothing is *wrong* with her. It's just, well, she's pregnant."

He blinked, his mind coming to a screeching halt. "She's... what?"

Melanie nodded. "Yeah, I'm guessing that's why she had Bernie take her to the clinic. The test results, anti-nausea meds, and prenatal vitamins were in her purse. I'm guessing you are the father?"

Blood roared in his ears at the term 'father'. He never once considered becoming one because what the hell did he have to offer a kid? The ability to teach them how to kill someone swiftly or painfully and get away with it? How to learn everything there was to know about their targets and stalk them from the shadows without being seen? None of that was even remotely conducive to raising a child.

Xavier only had two father figures himself, and neither had been good examples. His birth father was an abusive asshole with a drinking problem, who forced him to watch as he tortured and killed his mother. Rodrigo raised him to be a killer and taught him that emotions were a weakness. There was no way he would make a good father with them being his role models, and he was ashamed to admit it, but the thought terrified him. It was an odd feeling, too, because he wasn't scared of much.

However, the biggest concern was how Madelyn felt about becoming a mother. They hadn't been together long enough to have the whole 'kid' conversation, and he had planned on waiting until things settled down a bit between them before telling her how he felt about being a father. He wanted her to be able to make a sound decision on the subject.

Because she was a shifter's fated mate, she was more prone to having rambunctious shifter boys, and raising them was not for the faint of heart. Now, though, it was too late because she was already pregnant. The choice had been made for them.

There were now two lives he was responsible for.

Something on his face must have given away his thoughts because Melanie gasped, causing him to look up at her. "Well, what do you know," she commented in disbelief. "He has a heart after all."

His computer went off before he could tell her to go to hell, and both of them leaned closer to the screen.

"What's that? Did you find something?"

He shook his head. "No, it's an encrypted video call."

"Colby?" she asked, her voice hitching.

"Most likely."

"Well, why aren't you answering it?" she screeched, jumping up and reaching for the keyboard.

Xavier shoved her hands away instantly, and she was lucky that was all he did. He had already been barely holding it together, and with that new tidbit of information, his restraint was barely there.

"Damn it, Melanie. I have to set up a trace first. Unless you'd rather we *not* find Madelyn."

The detective huffed but kept her hands to herself, which was a good thing. He wasn't going to let anything cause him to miss this chance.

His fingers flew across the keyboard as he set up the trace. It only took him a few seconds, but it felt like a few seconds too many. When it came to finding his mate, every second counted.

Once everything was ready, he took a breath and answered the call.

Colby's irritating face appeared on the screen in front of him, and an involuntary growl escaped from deep within his chest. It was a cell phone camera, so it wasn't the best picture, but the guy was smirking as if he didn't have a care in the world and hadn't signed his own death warrant by taking Madelyn. At least, the scars on his face seemed to be causing him some pain.

"Where is she, Colby?" he ground out through clenched teeth.

"Well, hello to you too, Xavier," Colby replied, feigning offense. "Is that how your kind greets an old friend?"

Xavier shot to his feet so quickly that the chair clattered to the ground behind him as he slammed his hands on either side of his keyboard. "Goddamn it, Colby. Don't fuck with me right now. Where is she?"

Colby rolled his eyes and sighed in exasperation. "You

are no fun. You've always been that way too, always wanting to get right down to business."

The muscles in Xavier's jaw ticked as his eyes flashed and his claws began to extend. He wasn't going to be able to contain himself much longer.

"Oh, relax, would you? I got what you want right here."

He watched as Colby's arm disappeared off-screen before he pulled a bound and gaged Madelyn into view. Her cheeks were streaked with tears, and she was a little dirty, but she seemed to be otherwise unharmed. She was wearing a pair of sweats and the sweatshirt he had given to her the night she was attacked in the parking structure. Her eyes were puffy from crying, though she also seemed reluctant to look at him.

"Why don't you say hello, Madelyn?" Colby laughed, draping his arm around her shoulders. "He is, after all, why you are here and in this situation."

Chapter Twenty-Two

Madelyn

"**M**adelyn," she heard Xavier call to her through the video.

She closed her eyes at the sound of his voice so full of concern. A few stray tears rolled down her cheeks, soaking into the cloth wrapped around her head that was being used as a gag. She had cried so much since she had been taken that she was surprised her eyes hadn't dried out completely.

"Little dove, look at me."

Even though it pained her to do so, she hesitantly lifted her head to the camera and opened her eyes. She couldn't say no to him, and if this was the last time she was going to get the chance to see him, she was going to take it. Even if it was selfish of her. However, the sight of Xavier, the father of her unborn child, in his current state, nearly made her legs give out on her.

His face was covered in cuts and bruises, all in various

states of healing. His chest was the same, and she could only see that much because he was wearing a zip-up hoodie with no shirt underneath. Unfortunately, she couldn't see how bad the head wounds were due to the beanie he was wearing, and she could also tell that he was in a lot of pain even if he was trying to play it off that he wasn't, for her sake.

It also took her another moment to realize that he wasn't alone in, what seemed to be, a home office of some kind. However, it wasn't Isabelle who was with him, as she had expected. It was Melanie, which was an odd thing to see.

Instinctively, she wiggled her wrists, once again testing the zip ties that bound them together. Her hands were cold and a bit numb from them being on so tight. It wasn't enough to cut off her circulation completely, but it was enough to cause massive amounts of discomfort. Her lips and the inside of her mouth were dry as a bone from not being able to close her mouth, and she was filthy from all the times she had fallen on the hike up there from the service road. Colby and his guys had gotten a good laugh out of that too. Thankfully though, they hadn't touched her. At least, not yet. Somehow though, she knew that was about to change.

Madelyn had no idea what Colby had planned for her, but she knew that this video call to Xavier was a part of it. It had to be. And there was nothing she could do to stop it.

It had been a long time since she had felt this helpless. She had spent most of her life working her ass off to make it so that she never had to feel this way again too; hours of therapy, dozens of self-defense classes, and gun training. But it had all been for nothing. She didn't want anyone to see her like this, least of all Xavier, whom, she discovered, she had severely misjudged. Unfortunately, she didn't seem to have a choice.

Xavier's eyes flashed, drawing her attention back to him. He appeared to be struggling to remain calm. "Hey, baby. Y-you okay?"

Madelyn shook her head rapidly, her eyes filling with tears once more. Xavier didn't usually stutter, which further solidified how dire her situation was and amplified her fear and guilt.

Colby liked to hear himself talk, she had learned that over the last twenty-four hours. While she hadn't heard anything about what he was going to do with her, he hadn't stopped boasting about how he and the guys had nearly beaten Xavier to death the same night she had thought he had run back to Isabelle. The only thing that had stopped him from cracking Xavier's head open with a bat was Isabelle showing up with some former associates of theirs.

How messed up was that? She had thought the worst of him when he had been fighting for his life. That was another reason she couldn't face him. She didn't deserve to, and she would never forgive herself for thinking the worst of him.

Madelyn knew how this was going to go. Xavier was going to do whatever he could to get to her in time, and she couldn't let him do that. While she may only have a few hours left to live, she didn't want anything to happen to Xavier. However, with the gag in her mouth, she couldn't say anything at all to stop him.

"Oh, come on," Colby interjected, gripping the back of her neck and making her whimper. "She's fine. For now. But she's not going to stay that way, and I think you know that."

Xavier swiped his arm across the desk in front of him,

sending several things flying and making Melanie jump beside him. "Damn it, Colby. This is between you and me. She has nothing to do with this."

"It may have started out that way, but that's not the case anymore, is it?" Colby asked, cocking his head to the side. "Do you know how many of my guys were killed that night, thanks to Isabelle and those other assholes?"

As he spoke, his grip on her tightened, making her wince. She was definitely going to have bruises if he didn't kill her first.

Xavier's jaw clenched. "I didn't ask them to show up. I was ready to take all of you on myself, and you know that! What's it going to take, huh? Do you want me to give myself over to you? Done. Just tell me when and where, and for the love of God, let her go!"

Colby chuckled as he reached forward and brushed a strand of hair out of her face, the touch far too intimate for her liking. "It's too late for all that. The whole point of this call is to give you the chance to say your goodbyes."

"Colby, please!"

A sob escaped Madelyn's dry and cracked lips. She knew how hard that had to be, for Xavier to use the word 'please' as it wasn't in his usual vocabulary. She hated that Colby was using her to hurt him, and she wished more than anything that things were different.

Colby reached up and tugged the gag out of Madelyn's mouth. She winced at the pain as well as the relief of being able to finally close her mouth.

"Say what you have to say, sweetheart," Colby told her. "Because, once this gag goes back on, it stays on."

Madelyn looked back at the camera. There were so many things she wanted to say, so many words left unsaid both to Xavier and Melanie. But which of those things were the most important? What did one say when their time of death was rapidly approaching? She had never been good with words, and that obviously hadn't changed.

Licking her lips, though it didn't help much, she nodded mostly to herself. "I love you. Both of you," she began, her voice cracking and hoarse. "The two of you were the best things to ever happen to me, and I'm sorry that we didn't get more time."

"Madelyn, don't do that. Don't act like this is good-bye," Melanie sobbed, leaning over Xavier's shoulder. Xavier didn't even seem to mind, even though she knew how the two of them felt about each other.

"It is goodbye, Mel," she replied. "I wish it wasn't, but it is. I always knew my life was going to end something like this."

"No, it won't. I'm going to find you," Xavier growled. "I will always find you!"

"No!" she exclaimed quickly, shaking her head. She tried to take a step toward the camera, but Colby's grip prevented her from doing so. "You can't. You need… you need to save yourself, Xavier. You need to get as far away from here as possible."

Xavier gave her a sad smile. "I'm sorry, little dove, I can't do that. I can't live without you."

"Alright, time's up," Colby interjected. "Now it's time for me to show you the fun part!"

Xavier's eyes narrowed, but he didn't say anything, which made Colby's smile grow. Madelyn watched as Colby passed the phone off to one of the guys, a man she learned was named Richard.

"Now that you've said your goodbyes, I think it's time we get to the main event," Colby said almost cheerfully. Without waiting for a response, he once again grabbed her by the back of her neck and began leading her out of the room for the first time since she arrived.

The rest of the station was empty as they moved through it, though she could hear everyone outside. As they exited the back door, she blinked against the blinding bond fire they had going and nearly stumbled down the stairs because of it. Thankfully, Colby had a firm grip on her neck and was able to keep her upright.

It was a stormy night, and a few raindrops pattered against the top of her head, seemingly mirroring her current emotions. If either Xavier or Melanie said anything since they left the room, she couldn't hear over the cheers and hollers of the small crowd before them.

As they crossed the grass, the crowd parted, and what Madelyn saw behind them turned her blood cold and caused bile to rise in her throat. There, about three feet just outside the treeline was a freshly dug hole, and sitting beside that hole was an old refrigerator that was lying on its side with its lid open ominously. It wasn't hard to put the pieces together, and everything clicked in her mind. Colby planned on burying her alive and letting her suffocate to death.

What better way to torture Xavier than with the knowledge that she was suffering? She would be alone in the dark with only a few hours of oxygen at most. It would give him the slightest bit of hope that he would be able to find her in time, but then it would tear him apart on the inside when he discovered that he was too late. It always varied how long someone could stay alive when they were buried because it was contingent on how they were able to control their breathing. If people panicked, they had far less time than those who were able to remain calm in such a terrifying situation. She was definitely the former. There was no way she would be able to remain calm.

As soon as Madelyn realized the plan, she dug her

heels into the soggy ground. "No!" she screamed. "No! No, please!"

The crowd laughed at her pleading, every one of them looking giddy and excited. Monsters. They were all monsters, and she silently prayed to whatever god was listening that they all got what was coming to them.

Colby and another man she never caught the name of managed to drag her to the refrigerator despite her struggling. Colby spun her around to face the camera, gripping her jaw in one of his hands. Both Xavier and Melanie were screaming at the camera, and Melanie was sobbing, but Madelyn couldn't hear either one of them over the cacophony of noise. Nor could she look at them any longer.

"Say goodbye to the woman you love, Xavier!" Colby yelled loudly. "Because this will be the last time you see her alive! And then, I'm coming for you!"

With that, Colby and the other man lifted Madelyn off the ground and dropped her unceremoniously into the refrigerator. She landed face first, her arms slamming into the hard metal back. She cried out as pain seared through her whole body. She was pretty sure her shoulder had been dislocated, but her main concern was her baby as she had landed on her stomach fairly hard.

A sob wracked her body as she rolled over onto her back. She could see all of them crowding around to get a good look at her before they put her to death. Clint focused the camera on her face as he laughed and laughed while Colby reached out and grabbed the lid. The last thing she saw was the triumphant smirk on Colby's face as he slammed it shut, shrouding her in a never-ending darkness.

Once the lid was closed, everything else became muffled, and all Madelyn could hear was the rapid beating of her heart in her ears. Then, she was moving. She could feel the refrigerator being slid across the ground before she was finally shoved into the hole. Madelyn was thrown around the inside of her makeshift coffin like a rag doll, her head slamming into the sides before once again coming to a stop.

This was it. This was how she died. No matter what she did or how hard she fought, death was imminent, for both her and her baby.

Madelyn squeezed her eyes shut, pushing a few more tears down her cheeks as she began to mourn her child. They were going to die before they even had the chance to live. They wouldn't get to experience crawling or their first steps, they wouldn't learn how to drive or go to prom. It wasn't fair and she didn't understand how fate could be so cruel as to give her such a gift only to take it away just as quickly. But she guessed fate was a cruel bitch sometimes because, in just a matter of a few hours, she would be dead, and so would her child.

Chapter Twenty-Three

Xavier

The drive was taking way too damn long, and Xavier was nearly crawling out of his own skin. He was practically perched at the edge of his seat with his legs bouncing uncontrollably, not to mention the fact that his wolf was full of rage and aching to be set free.

The image of Madelyn being sealed inside the refrigerator, the terrified and helpless look in her eyes as Colby closed the lid and proceeded to bury her alive, was permanently burned into his mind. He was surprisingly nauseous, too, and more afraid than he had ever been in his life. He knew, without a doubt, that if they failed to reach Madelyn in time, if she was dead when they got to her, then he would have nothing left to live for and would probably end up taking his own life.

It didn't take much for them to learn that Colby was hiding out at an abandoned Ranger's station outside of town, and as soon as they figured that out, they were out the door. Xavier was sitting passenger while Melanie sat in the back so that he could keep an eye on her. He allowed Isabelle to drive only because he was in no position to do so in his current state.

The problem was that their destination was a little over three hours away. Every second that passed was another moment that could be Madelyn's last, which would mean the end of his child's life as well.

The more he thought about it, the more he was getting used to the idea of being a father. Even though it hadn't been planned, he helped to create a life instead of taking one. It was a novel thought, and he found that he actually wanted to see what it was like to be a dad.

The plan was simple, though he continued to go over it in his head just so that he would have something to do other than watch the scenery fly by. Melanie's job was to go for Madelyn immediately. He even had her bring a couple of shovels so that she didn't have to waste time looking for one. Meanwhile, while she was doing that, he, Isabelle, and the others were going to focus on taking out the threat. Rodrigo's crew was tasked with taking them out anyway, so they had a common goal. Everyone knew that Colby was his to kill though.

Xavier had no idea how this was going to play out, but he did know one thing: Colby and the assholes who had chosen to follow him were not going to survive the night.

His body was tense as he stared out of the passenger window, fighting tooth and nail to keep himself from shifting right there in the car. It didn't help that he could *feel* Isabelle looking over at him every few seconds, seemingly scrutinizing his every twitch and every shift in his seat. After over an hour of this, he had finally had enough.

"What?" he growled loudly, the volume of his voice shattering the quietness of the car and making both women jump. He couldn't be worried about their feelings right now though. He was barely holding it together. "What is your problem, Isa?"

"N-nothing," she stammered uncharacteristically. "I've just never seen you this tense before. You are usually more composed and put together before a job. It's fucking weird."

"This job is fucking different, you know that."

"Yeah, but why?" she asked bluntly. "I mean, what makes this girl so different from all the other girls you've banged?"

Xavier's jaw ticked as he ground his teeth together. He wasn't in the mood to try to explain it to her, nor did he see why he needed to. They no longer worked together and his relationship with Madelyn had nothing to do with her. Surprisingly, it was Melanie who decided to answer for him.

"Oh, haven't you heard? They're *fated mates.*"

Isabelle raised an eyebrow. "Am I supposed to know what that means?"

Through the side mirror, he could see Melanie roll her eyes. "It means they are soulmates. At least, that's what he says."

Isabelle let out a loud bark of a laugh, which was unlike anything he had ever heard from her before. He didn't think she could make that kind of sound, and even his wolf stopped raging inside of him for a brief moment.

However, the longer she laughed, the angrier he got again. The situation wasn't funny in the slightest. While Melanie had brushed Madelyn off when he asked for her after he woke up, he had thought that he set her straight about it. It was clear he had thought wrong.

"I'm sorry," Isabelle said after a while, running a finger beneath her eye to get rid of a bit of moisture there. "I don't mean to laugh, it's just, Xavier doesn't do serious, honey. Let alone soulmates. He tells girls what they want to hear so that they will spread their legs for him, but that's it."

Melanie snorted. "Are you sure about that? Because Madelyn's pregnant, so I'd say that's pretty serious."

At Melanie's comment, the smile dropped from Isabelle's face in an instant as her head snapped over to him. He just stared back at her, silently daring her to say something else stupid on the matter. He was dealing with a lot of pent-up frustration right now and had no problems using her as a verbal outlet. It wasn't like he had anything else to do while trapped in the car. He was just sick and tired of having to defend his relationship with Madelyn to everyone.

"Is… is she telling the truth?" Isabelle asked eventually.

He gave her a curt nod. "She is. Madelyn is pregnant with my kid. And she *is* my soulmate, Isa. I meant it when I said that I love her. I wasn't just saying that to convince Melanie to back off."

"Not that it would have worked," Melanie added.

"I see," was all Isabelle said before she pressed her lips together. Her grip tightened on the steering wheel, and the road before them seemed to become the most interesting thing in the world.

"Is that going to be a problem?" he asked.

Isabelle hesitated for a split second before she shook her head. "No, of course not. Why would it be?"

"I don't know," he responded. "You're the one acting like it's going to be."

"Nope. Not at all. There's no problem."

Xavier didn't believe her. There was something she wasn't telling him. Unfortunately, he didn't care enough to figure out what that was. He had other, more important things to focus on.

Once again, the three of them fell into an awkward silence as Isabelle continued to drive them toward their destination. While he was grateful the subject had been dropped, he hated that he no longer had that distraction. He was back to feeling like he was crawling out of his own skin and counting every second that passed them by in the blink of an eye.

"Oh my God," Melanie gasped with a soft laugh. He looked back at her to see what caused her to make such an exclamation, but her attention was solely on Isabelle. "You're jealous."

"What?" Isabelle scoffed. "No, I'm not. I know better than to bring a child into this dumpster fire. What Xavier does is his business."

Melanie shook her head and leaned forward in her seat. "No. Not that. I knew from the moment I met you that there was something between the two of you. I thought it was because you guys were sleeping together, but it's because you *want* to be. You are in love with Xavier."

Xavier huffed and expected Isabelle to deny it right away. It was ludicrous. However, when she didn't say anything at all, he looked over at her questioningly. She licked her lips before she met his eyes for a brief moment before focusing on the road again to make a right turn. The guys in the vehicles behind them followed closely.

"Oh, don't look so surprised, Xavier," Isabelle muttered. "Why do you think I showed up here and tried to get you to come back? Surely, you knew how I felt about you."

He hadn't known. He never once even suspected. He had thought she was like him, incapable of love. She used to say that to him all the time. Clearly, they *both* had been wrong as they had both fallen in love. It just wasn't with each other, at least, not on his part.

"You said your father was the one that wanted me back," he replied flatly.

Isabelle shook her head. "You know damn well if Rodrigo wanted you back, he wouldn't send me or anyone else to convince you to do so. He would do it himself."

"Isabelle—" he began. However, he didn't know what else to say.

Xavier never saw her that way. It was true that they had slept together many times over the years, but he thought she had known that sex was all it was to him. Sleeping with her had been a way to scratch the itch and nothing more. He never even considered her a sister even though they had been raised together. To him, she was just a murderer like he was.

"It's fine, Xavier," Isabelle said before he could figure out what to say to her. "I get it. Madelyn's your soulmate."

"I never meant to hurt you." The words felt lame, even to him, but they were all he could come up with. "I never knew you felt that way."

"Of course you didn't. Because I didn't want you to know and because you were so damn convinced that we couldn't have feelings because we killed people for a living. But like I said, it's fine. I'll get over it," she looked over at him then and gave him a small smile. "And for what it's worth, I'm happy for you."

"There's not going to be anything to be happy about if we don't get to her in time," he grumbled by way of response.

In that moment, Isabelle's feelings for him didn't matter. While it was a shocking revelation, he didn't return those feelings, and he never would. His heart and soul, if he even had those things, belonged to Madelyn alone. She was who was important to him.

Much to his surprise, Melanie reached over the passenger seat and patted his shoulder. "We will get to her in time, Xavier. We have to."

He silently sent up a prayer to whatever deity was listening that she was right.

Chapter Twenty-Four

Xavier

Dusk had fallen by the time they arrived at their destination, and Xavier had nearly lost his mind. He was anxious and antsy, and he was starting to lose control. Because of this, he was out of the car before it even came to a complete stop and was shaking with restraint and pacing while he waited for the others to climb out to meet him.

He *wanted* to leave now. No one knew how much air Madelyn had, and time was of the essence. His only thought was to get to his mate, but he had made the mistake of facing Colby, and the others alone before and he nearly lost his life because of it. He couldn't afford to make that mistake again, not when it was Madelyn's life on the line.

The service road they had pulled onto was lined with cars, most likely those that Colby and the others had been using to get around. They used their own cars to block them in. As soon as Melanie reached him, the two of them instantly bolted into the trees, unable to wait any longer. Behind him, however, he briefly heard Isabelle order a couple of guys to remain behind and disable the other vehicles. No one should be getting past them, but he could understand the need to take precautions. He wished he had done so earlier when it came to Colby. Then, maybe they wouldn't be in this mess in the first place.

Xavier shifted as soon as they stepped beneath the cover of trees, not caring one bit about shredding his clothing as there was a spare set in the backpack on Melanie's back. The good detective had also made sure that they had a first aid kit and some water as they had no idea what state Madelyn would be in when they finally got to her. The bag was also acting as a sheath of sorts for the two shovels they brought as well.

Usually, this would be the time when they hung back out of view to gather information and find the best way to eliminate their target, but they were forgoing all of that today. Not only were they working on a time constraint, but there wouldn't be any witnesses anyway. This was going to be nothing short of a slaughter, quick and easy, and as much as he wanted Colby to suffer, the urgency and need to get to Madelyn was far greater. It was also his sole focus as nothing mattered to him more than that.

Xavier's dark and twisted mind kept imagining the worst as he, Melanie, and the others darted quickly through the trees. His heart was racing, a pounding beat against his chest that matched the quickened pace of his paws against the forest floor. His mouth was dry, and his stomach churned dangerously. If he had been in human form, he would have been covered in a cold sweat. It took him a few moments to register that this was what panic felt like. He was afraid that they were too late and that

Madelyn would be dead by the time they got to her. However, even if that were the case, he wasn't going to stop until Colby and everyone stupid enough to side with him were dead. In his mind, they deserved nothing less.

The old ranger's station sat in the middle of a clearing. Xavier quickly surveyed the area while everyone got into position, surrounding the area so that none could escape, and what he saw threw him into a blind rage.

There were several small groups, all gathered around the various campfires they had started. They were drinking and laughing as if they didn't have a care in the world. No one would ever expect that they had buried a woman alive a short time earlier just by looking at them because they were actually enjoying themselves. However, not even fifteen feet away from them sat a freshly covered hole with a wooden cross shoved haphazardly into the ground above it. They had marked it as Madelyn's grave.

Xavier no longer cared if everyone was in position. They still had the element of surprise on their side, and he couldn't contain his rage any longer. He threw open the cage that usually bound his beast and gave in immediately as the monster took hold. His eyes blazed as he let out a roar that shook the trees and sent birds scattering into the sky above them. It was a warning to Colby and the others that death was coming for them.

Xavier's vision went red as he bound toward the group closest to him while Melanie hid behind a tree until they had taken down enough of the guys for her to safely get to Madelyn. Their fearful reactions made it clear that they didn't expect to be found so quickly.

He didn't even realize he had been airborne until his claws sunk into a guy's chest and they hit the ground hard. He made sure to curl his paws so that dislodging his claws caused an excruciating amount of pain as he rolled off the guy. He regained his footing quickly and was on his hind legs a moment later, his jaw clamping down around the man's neck. Cartilage and bone snapped beneath his powerful jaws as Xavier tore his throat out before he even had the chance to scream.

Gunfire broke out all over the clearing a moment later, both from his group and Colby's, and bodies were dropping left and right as they corralled the traitors into the middle, around the station. Xavier was lost to the beast inside of him, the one who had been locked up for way too long, and the taste of blood coating his tongue only fueled his need for revenge and to inflict pain. These guys had gone after the only thing in his life worth living for, and they deserved everything they got.

It was a bloodbath, unlike anything the small town of Cedarwood had ever seen. The ground was littered with the dead, and the grass was tinged red. A strong scent of copper and gunpowder filled the air, assaulting his senses. However, that was quickly replaced with the stench of burning hair and flesh as he used his massive paw to shove one of the guys into one of the campfires.

The screams that emanated from the man were inhuman and echoed through the area as he somehow got back to his feet despite the flames that completely engulfed him. He looked like a human fireball as he darted around the area in search of someone or something to help. Help never came for him though, and he continued to run, bits of his flesh melting off of him and falling onto the ground until the flames eventually killed him.

Small fires began burning the grass in his wake, and they spread quickly, making their job a little easier. After Isabelle and the others had seen how easily he had taken the guy out using the fire, they began to do the same thing, and soon, the whole area was filled with the pained wails of those being burned alive. A cloud of thick, dense smoke filled the clearing and burned his eyes, but it didn't stop his search.

Movement up by the station caught his attention, and he finally spotted Colby as he ran out the back door in an attempt to flee those who were now clearing the house. A wicked grin spread across Xavier's furry face as he changed direction and made his way toward the man who had started all of this.

Even with all of the conflicting scents in the air, Xavier could smell Colby's fear, and it made him giddy with excitement. He continued to stalk Colby until the man finally caught sight of Xavier's large wolf form and stopped dead in his tracks. Colby's eyes widened in fear and trepidation as Xavier shifted back to his human form.

"You fucked up, Colby," he sneered, slowly closing the distance between them. "You never should have gone after Madelyn. You crossed the line."

"You're… you're wasting your time with me, you know," Colby stammered, his eyes taking in the carnage around him. "I don't know how much oxygen that refrigerator has, you know. If you waste too much time, you're going to be too late. Then, no one will be able to help her."

"I'm aware. And I have someone taking care of that," he said simply, nodding over to the small mound of dirt where Melanie was digging. He had to give her credit too —she was making quick work of it.

Colby backed up a few feet and then suddenly pulled out a gun. Xavier rolled his eyes when Colby's hand shook violently as he pointed the weapon. With a supernatural burst of speed, Xavier closed the distance between them and snatched the gun out of Colby's hand. As he pressed the barrel underneath Colby's jaw, his other hand snapped Colby's wrist as if it were a toothpick.

"Haven't you learned by now that that shit doesn't work on me?" he asked over the sound of Colby's wails. "You took a bat to my skull, and I'm still alive and kicking. A gun isn't going to do shit."

"I had to try," Colby yelled, his cheeks streaked with tears and snot. "I'm so sick of you getting everything handed to you on a silver platter!"

Xavier laughed. "You think I had it easy? You don't know a damn thing about me or what I've been through, Colby."

"Xavier!" Melanie screamed, drawing his attention.

Somehow, the detective had managed to get Madelyn out of the refrigerator and laid her on the ground all on her own. However, Madelyn wasn't moving, which sent a dagger of fear into his heart.

Xavier growled low and looked back at Colby. "See you in hell, prick," he spat angrily. Colby's eyes widened a split second before Xavier pulled the trigger.

Before Colby's body even hit the ground, Xavier was sliding on his knees next to Melanie and the top of the refrigerator. Small rocks dug into his flesh, tearing his skin until he bled, but it didn't even phase him. It was the look on Melanie's face when she looked up at him that did.

"She's not breathing, and I can't find a pulse," she said urgently.

Tears filled his eyes as he looked upon the devastatingly beautiful face of his mate while Melanie began CPR. He could see the determination in her face, but he knew it was no use. Now that he had the chance to focus on it, he could tell that the shredded remains of their bond were already fading, which could only mean one thing: Madelyn was dead, and he would be soon too.

Chapter Twenty-Five

Madelyn

"No!" Madelyn suddenly screamed, yanking at the tubes and wires that were running up and down her arms.

Her nails clawed at her arms, attempting to dislodge the small, plastic tube that had wormed its way into her skin, while her other hand went to the one on her face that was trying to climb up her nose. At the same time, she kicked her legs widely to get the heavy piece of cloth off of them. She felt restrained, confined, and it only made her panic increase. Even the steady beeping up by her head was beginning to speed up.

"Whoa, it's okay, Madelyn," the oddly familiar voice said as a pair of hands gently grasped her flailing legs. "It's okay, you're safe now."

A second, larger pair of hands circled both of her wrists and pinned them down by her hips.

Madelyn blinked a few times, and the room she was in

finally came into focus. She wasn't still in the refrigerator as she originally thought. Instead, she was in a hospital room. The beeping was coming from the heart rate monitor. The tube she had torn out of her arm had been an IV and was now weeping blood down her arm, and she had a nasal cannula on her face providing her with a steady stream of oxygen.

Melanie was at the foot of the hospital bed, her hands on Madelyn's shins. She had dark circles under her eyes, messy hair, and wore disheveled clothes, but she was smiling at her with tears in her eyes.

"Breathe for me, little dove," a deep voice said from right beside her. Her gaze snapped to him as he released her wrists and placed a warm, calloused hand on the side of her face. "You gotta remember to breathe."

Licking her lips, Madelyn sucked in a deep, shaky breath. Her whole body ached, and it felt like she had been hit by a freight train, especially in her chest. If she was being honest, she felt like she had a couple of cracked ribs, though she didn't remember how she had gotten them.

As she looked between Melanie and Xavier, she discovered that she didn't want to believe that any of this was real because she feared that it was all just in her head. She was afraid it was some kind of death dream and that, when she woke up, she would still be inside that refrigerator, taking her last breaths. Or, maybe she was already dead.

Madelyn had never been more afraid in her life than when she was locked inside that refrigerator. It had been so dark and quiet that it nearly drove her mad. She remembered how the air began to thin and how hard it was to catch her breath and keep her eyes open. She had fought hard to stay awake, but sleep had taken her against her will, which was the last thing she remembered.

"Good girl," Xavier soothed after she did what she was told. "Take another deep breath for me."

With her eyes locked on his, she breathed again, and some of the panic finally began to dissipate. It was then that she realized that his arm was in a sling. The left side of his zip-up hoodie was only draped over his shoulder, and a fresh bandage was adhered to his skin.

"You're hurt," she croaked, her voice sounding weak and pitiful.

Xavier smirked. "I've had worse. It's just a scratch."

Melanie snorted then, drawing Madelyn's attention. "You're here," Madelyn said after a while. "You're *both* here."

"Of course *I'm* here," Melanie replied. "My best friend gets kidnapped by a psycho and buried alive while her stalker boyfriend sets out on a quest to get her back and crush everyone in his way? You can bet your ass I'm going to be there."

Madelyn laughed softly as tears formed in her eyes. The last time she had seen Melanie, she was screaming at her and calling her crazy for falling for her stalker. It appeared as though all of that had been forgotten, at least, for the moment.

"And there is not a single fucking place I'd rather be than right here with you," Xavier added as he splayed his hand across her abdomen. "And our baby."

Her heart skipped a beat, and the machine monitoring her heart rate betrayed it. "You know."

He nodded. "I know."

"How?"

He jutted his chin toward Melanie, which caused her brows to furrow. "And how did you find out?" she asked her friend.

"We found your purse in the parking lot of the clinic. It

had your test results and prenatals inside," Melanie answered, moving from the foot of the bed to the other side. "And I don't want you to worry. The doctor already said that everything looks good and the baby is fine."

"And C-Colby?" she asked, her voice cracking. "What about him?"

While she was beyond grateful that her baby was okay, it wouldn't matter if Colby was still out there. He would never stop coming for them and would always be a threat to them and their child.

"Hey," Xavier whispered. He pinched her chin between his fingers and pulled her attention to him. "You don't have to worry about him anymore, okay? He's gone."

"Really?"

Relief flooded her system as Xavier nodded and pressed his lips against hers before gathering her gently into his arms. "I love you, little dove. And I am so relieved that you are okay."

"I love you too," she whispered, a few more tears falling from her eyes.

"Oh, gag," Melanie teased softly, even though she seemed to be tearing up.

It seemed too good to be true; all of it did. It was hard to believe her fight with Melanie was over. She and Xavier were okay, Colby was gone, and both she and the baby were alive and well.

"In all seriousness though," Melanie began, causing Xavier to release her, "I'm sorry about before. I didn't know what was going on. I had no idea that you guys were fated mates, and I feel terrible about how we left things. Then you got taken, and I was afraid that something bad was going to happen to you, with you thinking I hated you."

"I never thought you hated me," she admitted. "I

just… hang on, how do you know that Xavier and I are fated mates?"

"I told her," Xavier said with a grin. "I was *trying* to convince her to stay away from Colby, but all it did was make her more determined."

"So, she knows that—"

"That the two of you are soulmates, that Xavier is a shifter, and that you are most likely carrying a shifter baby? Yup. I've been filled in on all the details," Melanie interjected. "It's a lot to get my head around, but I'm getting there. He seems to be completely devoted to loving you and keeping you safe, so we are good. For now."

"Appreciate it," Xavier chuckled.

Madylen shook her head in disbelief but couldn't keep the smile off her face. Her best friend and boyfriend were getting along. She never thought she'd see the day.

Taking a moment to get a look around the room, she realized that many of the flat surfaces were full of flowers, stuffed animals, and balloons. It almost looked like a gift shop, given how many there were in such a small, confined space.

Following her gaze, Melanie smiled at her. "From everyone at the station," she told her. "They send their love and want you to get better soon."

"And I'd like to add a few more from the Cortez family," an unfamiliar, female voice said from by the door. "If you don't mind."

Madelyn looked over to see a gorgeous redhead stepping inside the room. She was wearing a pair of ridiculously tight jeans, a black shirt, boots, and a black leather jacket. In one arm, she was holding a huge basket full of all kinds of things, and in the other, she held a small gift bag and a stuffed wolf.

Xavier was on his feet in an instant, positioning himself

between her and the newcomer. "What are you doing here, Isabelle?" he growled in warning.

Madelyn blanched. *This* was the woman Xavier hooked up with?

"Oh, relax, Xavier. I come in peace," Isabelle stated, brushing him off. "You know I had to come meet the girl who stole your heart. And I brought gifts."

Isabelle rounded the bed, all three of them staring after her in both surprise and disbelief. She set the basket in one of the chairs that wasn't being used before turning back to face her. If Madelyn didn't know any better, she would say that Isabelle appeared to be a little nervous.

"It's nothing too crazy," Isabelle rambled on. "It's just some skin and hair care products, a couple of different kinds of coffee, and some chocolate of course. Because you can never go wrong with chocolate. And these," she held up the stuffed wolf and small gift bag. "Are for the little one."

Madelyn hesitantly took the gift bag and opened it. Despite her confusion about meeting Isabelle for the first time and seeing how gorgeous she was, a smile spread across her lips when she saw what was inside. It was a tiny black hoodie just like the ones Xavier always wore.

"I figured the kid was probably going to be a lot like its father," Isabelle commented. "But if you don't like it—"

"It's perfect," Madelyn interjected.

Melanie laughed. "Yeah, it kind of is."

"Thank you, Isabelle. You didn't have to do this."

"I know that you and I got off on the wrong foot," Isabelle replied. "I knew what you thought when you called that day, and I didn't bother correcting you. For that, I'm sorry. But the fact of the matter is Xavier is family, whether he wants to be or not, which means that you and this baby are too. And we take care of family."

"So, I take it your father knows we worked together to take down Colby and rescue Madelyn?" Xavier asked, folding his arms across his chest.

Isabelle smiled. "You know there's no keeping anything from him. He knows everything. He also said to give you this along with his congratulations on the newest member of your family." She then pulled a letter out of her back pocket and passed it over to Xavier.

Madelyn didn't know how she felt about Xavier's old boss being so informed about her life. Melanie even met her gaze and lifted an eyebrow in question.

While Xavier read the letter he had been given, Isabelle stepped up to the side of the bed. "You're good for him, Madelyn. You change him for the better, and I am really happy for the two of you."

"You are?" Madelyn asked, unable to stop herself.

The redhead nodded. "Really. Take care of him, yeah?"

"I will," she promised.

Isabelle patted her leg and quickly took her leave.

Once she was gone, Melanie blew out a breath and ran her fingers through her hair. "Well, that wasn't weird or anything."

Madelyn laughed weakly. "My life has seemingly become all sorts of weird lately."

"And, it just got weirder," Xavier added, passing her the letter. "Rodrigo set up a trust fund for the baby and gave us a shit-ton of money. He said he wants to make sure we are taken care of. He also said that he and the rest of the family will make sure that we are safe to live out the rest of our lives in peace and that, if we ever need anything, not to hesitate to give them a call."

That really threw her for a loop. From what Xavier had said previously, once someone left the family, that was it.

They were completely cut off. She suspected that Rodrigo saw Xavier as more of a son than he realized. It was the only explanation he had for what the guy had done for them.

When Colby had locked her in that refrigerator, Madelyn thought her life was over. She never expected to be saved, nor did she expect any of this. It was everything she had ever wanted but never thought she'd have. She had not had the best start to her life, but things were finally looking up. Her life was changing for the better, and that was all thanks to her stalker, the man she had grown to love, and her best friend, who stuck by her side, no matter what. Without the two of them, she and her baby wouldn't be alive.

Madelyn no longer saw darkness around every corner and now knew what true hope and happiness felt like. It was a feeling she was going to cherish for the rest of her long life.

Chapter Twenty-Six
A FEW DAYS LATER

Xavier

Every instinct he had ever had was screaming at him, making his skin itch while setting his wolf on edge. He didn't want to be here. It was too public, too exposed, and there were way too many cops around.

Just a few months ago, he wouldn't have been caught dead at a cop's funeral, but this wasn't for him. He was here for his mate and because he was trying to be better, for her. She was the only one who could make him do things that he otherwise wouldn't do. Bernie had been her friend, and he had died trying to protect her. In his eyes, the man had earned his respect, but he wasn't going to lie and say that he wasn't glad that the thing was finally over.

Madelyn had managed to convince the doctor to release her early so that she could attend the funeral because it had been that important to her, and they had come directly from the hospital. Melanie had even brought them both something to wear so that they didn't have to make a stop. In the beginning, he had wanted to insist that Madelyn stay in the hospital until she was actually released, but he managed to restrain himself even though it wasn't easy.

Xavier stood protectively behind Madelyn as she said her goodbyes over the casket. The other attendees had already left, leaving the two of them alone by the gravesite. Even so, he couldn't stop himself from scanning the area for any signs of trouble. It was a habit that was drilled into him from a young age. Because of this, he was able to spot Melanie as she made her way back to them. At the same time, Madelyn kissed the tips of her fingers and pressed them against Bernie's casket, a few tears rolling down her cheeks.

He knew that she felt responsible for Bernie's death. She had told him so when she had recounted what transpired with Colby, but he wished that she wouldn't. It wasn't her fault, and even Melanie had told her that. Unfortunately, nothing they said seemed to change her mind, and he could feel her guilt as easily as if it were his own.

"Rest easy, Bernie," she whispered before stepping back next to him and taking his hand.

Gripping her hand securely in his, they rounded the gravesite to meet up with Melanie.

"Are you sure you don't want to come to the reception?" she asked as they approached.

Madelyn shook her head. "I'm sorry. I'm just exhausted, Mel. And I haven't been home in days. There's just… there's a lot I need to process."

"Like being pregnant with a shifter baby?" Melanie teased her gently.

The corner of Madelyn's lips turned up slightly. "Yeah, that's definitely part of it."

"Alright, well, give me a call if you need anything."

Madelyn hugged Melanie and promised to do so should the need arise. Because of everything she had gone through, her boss had given her some medical leave, and he had every intention of making sure that she rested the whole time. She deserved it.

As they went their separate ways, Melanie gave him a single nod, and he did the same. They still weren't the biggest fans of each other, but they were being civil for Madelyn's sake. Maybe, one day, the two of them would become friends, but today was not that day.

After helping Madelyn into the car, he climbed in behind the wheel and pulled out of the cemetery. The atmosphere was tense, but he knew that he wasn't the one she was angry or upset with. She was just dealing with a ton of emotions on top of hormones due to the pregnancy. Situations like this were what made him glad he was a bit emotionally stunted. He wouldn't know how to process all of that either.

As they turned onto the main road, he reached over to take her hand in his again. "Are you okay, little dove?"

"No," she admitted, glancing over at him. "But I will be. I just need a little bit of time to get my head around everything that's happened. That's all. A lot has happened the last few days."

He nodded as he made a turn. "Well, don't worry. I'll make sure you get plenty of time over the next few weeks."

"Uh, Xavier? This isn't the way to my house."

A smirk spread across his lips. He had been waiting for her to notice that he wasn't taking her back to her old place. It had taken a lot of late-night calls to Melanie while Madelyn was sleeping, and he now owed the good detective a lot of favors, but it was worth it. While he *was* trying to be a better man for her, there were just some inclinations that he couldn't get rid of.

"It is now. You're moving in with me, Madelyn. You are my mate and the mother of my child. This whole living apart shit isn't going to work for me anymore."

He had expected many different reactions after telling her that he was essentially moving her in with him, but he didn't expect her to laugh about it. It wasn't the kind of laugh she made when she couldn't believe something either. It was a genuine laugh that made him smile.

"You know, I should be surprised and upset that you just assume that I'm going to move in with you now," she stated. "But I'm not. It seems like the next logical step."

"We could get married, too, if you'd like," he teased.

"Don't push it, Xavier," she retorted. "But why your place? Why not mine?"

"Easy," he replied. "There's more room for me to run when I need to, and there are fewer people around, so it's less likely for someone to stumble across me in wolf form. Our child is going to need that same space and seclusion after they are born."

"I guess that makes sense," she muttered. "I just wish you would have given me a heads up or, at least, stopped by my place so I could grab some things."

"Everything you need is already at home," he told her.

She laughed again. "How on earth did you manage that?"

"Let's just say I owe Melanie a few favors," was all he said in response.

He could feel her studying him for several moments before she spoke again. "You… you seem different."

He cocked an eyebrow as he looked over at her. "Different how?"

She shook her head. "I don't know. You seem…less intense somehow. More…"

"Human?" he provided. When she didn't say anything else, he just shrugged. "I'm trying something new. I'm trying to be better. For you."

The hand he was holding gently squeezed his. "You don't need to change for me, Xavier. I know the kind of man you are, I always have. And I fell in love with you anyway."

Lifting their joined hands, he pressed a kiss to her knuckles. "I know, and I love you for that. But I don't feel like I *have* to change, little dove. I *want* to. I want to be the man that you and our child deserve. I know I can't change who I was in the past, or what I've done, but I can change the present and the future."

"Does this mean you are going to stop being so protective of me?" she asked playfully.

He narrowed his eyes. "Yeah, not a chance. It's probably going to get worse now that you are pregnant too. So, you may as well get used to it."

This wasn't what he was used to, having someone he loved so much he couldn't imagine life without her. He wasn't used to having something worth losing, but Madelyn was both of those. The thought of that scared him, but she was worth it. She was his smile, his breath of fresh air. She was the one who brought him out of the darkness and into the light. Without her, he was nothing, and he was going to spend the rest of his life showing her how much she meant to him if it was the last thing he did.

he End

Dear Reader

I hope you enjoyed this story! Please take a moment and leave a review for the next reader.

I love connecting with my readers! Please feel free to follow me on any or all platforms:

Amazon: https://www.amazon.com/Amanda-K-Mann/e/B08T6122GY

Goodreads: https://www.goodreads.com/author/show/21091321.Amanda_K_Mann

Bookbub: https://www.bookbub.com/profile/amanda-k-mann

FB: https://www.facebook.com/amandakmannauthor

Join My Readers Group: https://www.facebook.com/groups/159222315736563

Instagram: https://www.instagram.com/amandakmannauthor

About the Author

Amanda K. Mann is from California, born and raised. She's the mother of two amazing children, both a son and a daughter, and a Marine wife, which means she moves to a new home every three years or so.

Besides being an animal lover and Supernatural addict, she spends most of her free time with her nose stuck in a book or typing away at some new idea that pops into her brain. Her blood type is caffeine, and she is a sucker for cute otter pics.

You can follow Amanda on Amazon, Bookbub, Facebook, Goodreads, or Instagram.

For more information about her published works, visit www.amandakmann.wordpress.com